MW00747868

ISBN 9780993696107

Book design by Margot McLaren

Also by David Slater:

The Biscuit Barrel
The Samurai's Son
Dirges & Doggerel – Collected Verse

Acknowledgments:

A great big thank you to John Wright, Chuck and Lynn Ingram, Jim Place, Michael Fitch and Lisa Shantz whose no-nonsense editorial input into the content of this book was so important.

I must also acknowledge the help of Bob Bell for his technical advice on gold extraction methods.

David Slater

The Warthog's Tusk

ʹΕΔ

Opusdavey Press

For Aletta

'....you're that lovely long-stemmed rose, I am the sharpest thorn,

I am the darkest, deepest night, you are the fragrant dawn'

The young man was trembling with excitement and anticipation. He lurched in the nine o'clock darkness, his feet stumbling on small bushes and clumps of grass. The starlight from a cloudless African sky faintly illuminated the huge granite boulder that was his goal. Alongside it he could see the dark smudge of the ironwood tree. Nearly there, and he felt again the surging of excitement in his chest.

The anticipation he felt was sexual in nature; he had read the girl's note with great excitement. He could almost see her in the gloom ahead. He started to imagine the warmth of her, the smell of her, the soft whimperings of pleasure. His breath was shortening, nearly there and he was panting, not from the exertion but from passion.

Suddenly he heard Isobel whisper: "Gideon. Is that you?"

And then he saw her in the star-shadow of the grey-green ironwood tree, and she beckoned him forward with her arms open wide.

At almost the same moment he felt a hard object strike him on the back of his head and he collapsed on the soft grass, his brain unable to comprehend what had happened to him. As he lay on the sandy ground, slowly recovering his senses, he felt a sharp pain in his buttocks, a pain akin to a stabbing. Not once, but twice, and then a third time. And then he felt himself being turned over onto his back and he felt the knife going into his groin.

In less than three minutes he was dead.

Chapter 1

Tabora, Tanganyika, November, 1918

"Parade! Parade! Atten...'shun!"

The sound of a thousand boots hitting the parade-ground's hard-packed clay in perfect unison created a reverberation that brought nothing but joy to Regimental Sergeant Major Samuel Kumalo's heart. He stood tall and as straight as a rod under the early summer, scorching hot East African sun, proudly wearing his Sam Browne belt, his highly burnished pace-stick glinting brightly in its rays.

His khaki uniform had been starched and ironed by his batman early that morning before the sun had cast its first pink ray in the east. Its brass buttons had been burnished to an eye-squinting brightness. On his head he wore his red fez with black silk tassel at a rakish angle on his head. The polished brown fez-strap was worn tight, barely under his chin. And on his feet, underneath those khaki puttees tied so meticulously around his shins, were his hob-nail boots. Here again, his batman had done him proud. His boots had been boned to a shine that even the white officers were envious of. He could easily have been the poster-boy for Kiwi polish.

He was so very proud of the men standing to attention on the parade-square in front of him. These were *his* men, *his* boys. He considered them his children, not in any paternalistic way, but rather because he had trained them all. He had sculpted them from frightened, skinny, half-fed village youngsters into a fighting force that even the Grey Ghost himself, Lettow-Vorbeck, the German military commander, feared more than any other he had faced in East Africa. Feared more than the turban-clad Indians whom he had mown down by the hundreds with well-placed ambushes in the forests above the bloody, bee-infested, Indian Ocean beaches at Tanga. Feared more than the sallow, pimple-faced Portuguese conscripts who had cowered in their redoubts and their forts deep in Mozambique. Feared even more than the white South Africans and Rhodesians, like Selous and Smuts. Oh yes, his boys had made a reputation for themselves! Fearless in battle, tireless on the march. He had fought with them, cursed at them, led them on lunatic charges against impossible German positions. And every loss of one of his men he felt personally, like a cold hand reaching into his chest and tearing at his very heart.

Oh yes, these were *his* boys.

Samuel remembered with pride that week in late November 1917 when he had force-marched his boys for a week towards Negomano as they chased Vorbeck over the Rovuma River into Mozambique. For three days his men had not eaten a morsel, nor lit a fire that might betray their positions to the German quarry.

That man Lettow-Vorbeck! What a clever, wily general he had proven to be. Never beaten in battle, with his force of mainly black askaris, never totalling more than 20,000, he had tied up well over 200,000 British and allied troops. If those latter forces could only have been released to Western Europe, how much sooner might the Great War have come to an end? Or perhaps, how much greater would the slaughter in the trenches of Western France have been?

But now that brutal, bloody, inch-by-mud-slimy-inch war *was* at an end. An armistice had been signed in far-off Europe. Lettow-Vorbeck had received a telegram from his superiors in Germany, three days in reaching him, informing him of the armistice. And now he and his rag-tag army, his undefeated army, were in Abercorn in Northern Rhodesia, ready to surrender to that seven foot giant of a South African soldier, General Jacob Van Deventer.

Samuel had a feeling that his life would now be changing yet again. Hardly a day went by that he did not wonder what had happened to his *ubaba*, his mentor, his friend, Hastings Follett. He had last seen him in 1917 in Arras, France, shortly before Follett went off to join the Royal Flying Corps. Samuel still felt badly that he had not been able to see his friend again, face-to-face as old friends do, that he had had to resort to sending Hastings a letter to tell him of his hasty departure for East Africa.

For 'departure' rather read 'strategic retreat', because
Samuel knew that if he had not left France when he did he
was quite certain he would have been killed. The white
South Africans never take kindly to a black man pointing a
finger at one of their own. Especially when that finger
spells *murder*. He had left the day after those two South
African officers had been arrested by British Military
Policemen. He never did find out if there had been a trial,
but he was confident that the file he had handed over to the
MPs was complete in every way, full statements from
witnesses, signed and independently witnessed, a hundred
different pieces of evidence, all logged and tagged, in the
very precise way he had been taught at The Depot, back in
far away Rhodesia. They were guilty as sin, those two, had
even bragged to their fellow mess-members about the
beating they had given that poor Cape Malay, Henny
Boesman. But of course in the eyes of their fellow officers
they were innocent, the beating merely a just reward for the
crime of 'giving lip'. And, yes, the 'Capie' had been
drunk, barely understandable, pissed out of his mind on
cheap rot-gut brandy smuggled in from South Africa on
one of the transports. But did that justify a man's life?
Any man's life? And these same brother officers had sworn
to get even with Samuel Kumalo.

He had been glad to get back to Africa, for homesickness
had been a constant companion. He had tried as hard as he
could to get leave to visit his family in Bulawayo. But no,
his troopship, sailing north from the Cape of Good Hope
had steamed right past Beira, where he might have caught
the train for some home leave. The first land he set foot on

after leaving France was at Mombasa, in British East Africa.

And Agnes Nyatoti, the love of his life, shebeen-queen and talented brewer of *doro,* daughter of a mine captain at the Rezende Mine in Penhalonga, Manicaland, would just have to wait another year, perhaps even another two years, wait for this terrible white man's war to be over.

§

But now the parade was at an end, the men dismissed, and the brigadier's speech still rung in two thousand ears. Most of those ears hadn't understood a word of it all. All the bullshit of how the King was so grateful to them for all the hardships they had endured, how the world was now a safer place and so on, ad nauseam. How the hell did King Georgie know? The few times he'd set foot outside of England during the four years while the war raged had been to visit army campsites well to the rear of his soldiers' miserable, foot-deep-in-water, rat-infested trench-lines. No, Samuel's men didn't understand the high-flown words. He would tell them later, in their ten different native languages and dialects, around the cooking fires as they ate their last supper of maize-meal porridge and boiled meat and kale together before boarding an early morning train for Dar-es-Salaam and then onward to their far-flung homes.

It had been Colonel Hicks, the administration adjutant, who, just before the parade assembled, had handed Samuel the buff envelope with his orders. Somewhere within all those typewritten words on a cheap piece of government paper marked OHMS, was the message that he should move as soon as possible to Dar-es-Salaam, there to board ship for Beira. Upon disembarking in Beira he was to take the first available train for Salisbury, and there to report for duty at Police General Headquarters. He would then be formally de-mobilized from the King's African Rifles and re-enlisted into the ranks of the British South Africa Police. Rank: Askari. Four years of hard fighting for King and Empire and *this* was his reward? Re-enlistment at the same rank as when he had left for overseas service? It just didn't seem fair. Had they no idea that he was now a Regimental Sergeant Major? No idea that before he left for the war he had passed the police corporal's examination with distinction? No idea that he was of Matabele royal blood?

As badly as this letter rankled, Samuel was mollified by the fact that, according to the same scrap of paper, upon demobilization he would be the recipient of a grand total of two hundred and four pounds sterling. He had drawn very little in the way of pay while in France, although God knew there had been so many temptations on which to spend it. Ah yes! How well he remembered those French girls in Arras and Ypres and Cambrai. So accommodating, so skilled in their profession, and yet never once asking for payment for their deliciously precious time. Fancy-man they called him, their *prince noir*. Was it his colour that had so intrigued them? Or the sensual wildness of a Matabele warrior? And then after he arrived in East Africa he had again drawn almost nothing. He had hardly been in a base camp long enough to do so.

Oh, and *bien sur*, don't forget the medals. There would be three medals coming to him in due course: one for just being a soldier, like every other one of the King's six million bags of flesh and bone, plus a bronze medal for his service in France in the native labour battalions. And then finally, one for the East African campaign. Two of them made with high quality silver with King Georgie's bearded face on one side and St. George on his horse on the other, a lance cradled in his arm, a dragon trampled underfoot. The field commendation for his 'bravery in the face of the enemy' that he had received at Schuckmannsburg in the Caprivi in 1914 meant nothing. He had been classed as a supernumerary at the time, polite words for 'lower than dog-shit' in the eyes of the military. If he had been a white officer he would probably have been awarded a Victoria Cross or at least a Military Cross. But Schuckmannsburg was a nothing battle in the overall scheme of things and so Samuel had received a piece of vellum. He had opened it but once, to show Hastings. And even Hastings, the very man whose life he had saved at Schuckmannsburg, that German post on the banks of the Zambezi, had snorted with derision.

§

On the one week voyage, by rail, then sea, then rail again, he occupied his mind with thoughts of what he would do with his money. There should be enough to buy a small farm, he thought, a few head of cattle, and to cover *roora* or bride price. He was now twenty-eight. He thought it was high time that he married. He had a very good idea who that bride might be. Oh yes, it could only be Agnes, if she

would have him. A very enterprising young lady, well
trained in the art of brewing traditional African beer, *doro*,
using only the finest brown millet, as well as *hwahwa*, a
beer made from ground white maize. Her father worked at
the Rezende Mine in Penhalonga, a shift-boss, a man of
stature in the community. It was true that she was not of
Samuel's tribe, not a Matabele, but he could forgive her
that transgression, her accident of birth. She more than
made up for it with the wonderful beer that she brewed.
Agnes was a *Samanica*, the eastern offshoot of the Vashona
tribe, and her father owned a big spread in the Honde
Valley, up Inyanga way, farmed by two of his younger
brothers while he toiled in the gold-mine. No, it wasn't all
bad. And he knew she had loved him when he left for the
war. He just hoped that she loved him still. After all, he
had been away for four long years, and Samuel, with an
insight gained from being around young soldiers with girls
in far off places, knew only too well what time and distance
can do to a relationship.

Chapter 2

Salisbury, Rhodesia, December, 1918

"Two weeks, Kumalo," said the PGHQ staff adjutant. "That's it, two weeks. You'd better be back here on January 2nd or I'll post you AWOL. Is that understood?"

Samuel understood. Oh yes, he understood only too well. Understood that his service overseas meant absolutely bugger-all to these desk-Wallas. Understood that in his absence, men with less service time had been promoted above him. And, yes, it hurt. Like a dagger in the back, it hurt. But the hurt wouldn't stop him from enjoying the next two weeks.

§

Umtali hadn't changed much in the four years he had been away.

He had passed through the town on his way up from Beira, after his ship had landed him from Dar-es Salaam, but there hadn't been time to get off and look around. Now he was back in the pretty town set in a hollow in the mountains, bougainvillea flowering profusely in every garden. Jacaranda trees lining the broad avenues. But Samuel had little regard for the pretty gardens. He had his mind set on transportation, or rather, his lack thereof. How on earth was he to get to Penhalonga, fifteen miles away? Yes he could walk, but what he really needed, he thought, was a bicycle. He thought of his options: buy or borrow? He felt the wad of notes and heavy mound of sovereigns in his pocket. How much lighter would it have been had he invested in that Rudge he had seen in Raj Patel's shop window on Railway Avenue back in Salisbury. Twelve pounds Raj had wanted. Twelve pounds for a shiny, black, 28 inch marvel of Birmingham engineering. And with a chrome-shiny rear carrier thrown in as a bonus! But his better sense had prevailed and he had merely window-shopped in Salisbury, despite the very close attention and toothy smiles of the Indian traders whose gaily-festooned general stores lined the north side of Railway Avenue from one end to the other. He could still smell the coal-smoke from the Garrett locos chuff-chuffing in the station opposite.

§

Now he walked the small distance from Umtali station to the police encampment, a kit bag slung over his shoulder.

"Name?" asked the askari on guard at the pole gate. Samuel sighed. These new boys, he thought, how little they know. Four years ago they would have been standing to attention as I walked through the gate, but now, nothing. Not even a

15

glimmer of recognition. *What on earth is the world coming to?* he thought with a sigh, not for the first time.

"My name is Kumalo, Samuel Kumalo."

The young guard looked very closely at the tall-well-muscled man standing before him. He noted the tribal markings on either side of his broad nose which meant that he was not from these parts, and his accent betrayed a hint of Shangaan or Matabele, maybe even Zulu. But he also noted a certain aura about the man which spoke of command, self-certainty, inner strength.

"And what is your business here?"

"I am here to see the Commanding Officer. Superintendent Spencer Thorneycroft." This is a cheeky little bugger, thought Samuel.

The young policeman scanned his clipboard. "I have no information to show that you are expected."

"Just phone through to his office and tell him that Samuel Kumalo is here." The young policeman caught something in the tone of the visitor's voice which suggested that the big man was not someone to be trifled with.

§

"Well I never! Samuel Kumalo! How very good to see you, Samuel. Sit down, you must tell me all about your war." Thorneycroft grasped Samuel's hand and they did the traditional three-part shake. Though Thorneycroft was the commanding officer for Manicaland, one of the most senior government men in the province, he had never lost the human touch. He was a dark man, wiry black hair now specked with silver, cut very short, lean of body and tough as nails He was genuinely glad to see Samuel. He would have loved to have gone to war himself, but he had been well over forty years old when war broke out in August 1914. Besides, he had been badly wounded in the Boer War twenty years earlier and his leg still gave him a lot of pain, especially when the weather was cold and damp.

"Sir, I will tell you everything, but first I was hoping you could help me with the loan of a police bicycle? I am on two weeks leave and I need to get down to Penhalonga, to Mr. Evans' mine, and it will be easier if I can go by bike."

"Bicycle? Bloody hell, man, after what you did for Trooper Follett in the Caprivi, I can't let you ride a bicycle! Did Follett ever teach you to ride the Indian motor-cycle?"

"Oh yes, sir. I became quite good at riding it. And in France I also rode, delivering messages and despatches, but not an Indian, it was a Royal Enfield, from England. Sir, I have been meaning to ask. To which station has Mister Follett been posted?"

Thorneycroft looked dumbfounded. "You haven't heard?"

"What, sir, haven't heard what? We received no mail in East Africa. And when I enquired at GPHQ, they told me to make enquiries in Umtali, since that was Mr. Follett's last post."

"No, I suppose being out in the bush for as long as you have been, you wouldn't have had any news at all. Well,

Kumalo, I'm terribly sorry to have to tell you this, but Follett didn't make it. He was shot down in his plane on March 10th of this year. They said it was some new-fangled German invention called anti-aircraft fire. I'm so, so, sorry, old chap, I know how closely you worked with him, how well the two of you got on."

Samuel was stunned by this news. For a moment he was speechless, could do nothing but sit there thinking about his old boss, his friend, his 'small father' *ubaba* as he'd called him in the letter he had written Hastings as he was leaving France for Africa. And he remembered the cases they had worked on together, the gold thief, Justice Sibanda, whose death they had at first thought to be accidental but was really a very clever poisoning. And Vlok and Meyer and that poor Indian fellow, Gulabh, who had lost his life to Vlok's Mauser bullet and half his leg to a crocodile. Oh *ubaba, bayete Inkosi.* I salute you great chief!

§

It was not the same Indian motor-cycle that Samuel and Follett had ridden four years earlier. This one was a newer model, probably American war surplus, the red paint now a drab army olive green. Not very gallant, thought Kumalo, but definitely better than pedalling the fifteen miles out to the Rezende Mine. And far, far better than walking!

It had rained the previous day and the road was slick with mud. Nonetheless, the Indian handled very well on the muddy road. Nothing much had changed since the last time he had travelled this road, still the same bone-numbing corrugations and the long ribbon-lakes of water in the low

18

areas. He was getting muddier by the minute, but it was still a lot better than the alternative.

And then, suddenly, he had to brake sharply, the rear wheel fish-tailing wildly beneath him. A family of guinea-fowl, a worried, grey-speckled mother hen and eight tiny chicks crossed the road in front of him. As he picked up speed again, the danger past, he smiled as he thought back to his childhood in Lupane in far away Matabeleland. He couldn't have been more than six or seven. Wandering through the bush one day he had surprised just such a mother-to-be, sitting on a clutch of eggs. They were a brownish colour, speckled and sharply pointed at one end, but otherwise looked very much like a domestic chicken's eggs. He had taken four of the eggs, all that he could hold in his two small hands, and brought them proudly back to his mother. She had been pounding maize kernels in her well-worn hollowed-out grinding log. She stopped her pounding long enough to inspect the eggs, holding each one carefully to her ear.

"Quick, *umntanami,* put these eggs under that broody hen over there. Unless I am mistaken you should soon have four fine guinea-fowl chicks."

And his mother had been right. When the eggs hatched a few days later, the old brood-hen had been the proud mother of nine fluffy little chicks, and although four were completely different in colouration, she loved every one of them the same.

He smiled when he thought of his mother and how she had called him 'little one'. Even the last time he had seen her, at Lupane Station on his long journey back from the Caprivi nursing a delirious, wounded Hastings Follett, she had called him *umntanami* – and he a six foot, three inch, two hundred pound warrior!

And now the motor-cycle's front wheel was jack-hammering his hands to numbness, and he thought back to the last time he had travelled this same road. He and Hastings on the old Indian with its one-wheeled side-car, flying along in a cloud of yellow-brown dust. Samuel couldn't help but feel guilty; guilty that he should be the one returning from a bitter four years of hard fighting without even a scratch, while Hastings lay in a grave in Rue Petillon Cemetery. He missed his old friend and comrade in arms, missed him so, so much.

§

He found his way to Agnes' father's small house, neat and built of fired brick with a corrugated iron roof, rather than pole and mud with a thatched roof like most of the others. Agnes' father had status. He was one of three foremen, each running a mining crew of forty men working underground in the tunnels that latticed the earth beneath their feet.

"*Masikati,* Agnes. *Maswerasei?*" What charming people these Shona people are, thought Samuel. First they say 'good afternoon' and then they ask, 'how did you spend your day?' And, if true to her people's hospitable form, Agnes should respond:

"Masikati. Ndaswera kana maswerawo." 'I spent my day well, if you spent your day well.'

Except Agnes didn't say that. She looked up from the large oval galvanized-zinc tub in which she was washing clothes, a bar of green Sunlight soap in one hand, her mouth firmly closed in a grimace that could only be evidence of anger. Then she collected herself, dropped the soap with a big *ker-plop* into the sudsy water, wiped her foamy hands on the ample sides of her bright yellow and green cotton dress and walked right up to Samuel. She looked at him quizzically, initially straight into his wide, hairless face, marked on either side of his broad nose with tribal tattoos, then up and down his tall, powerful body. Then she walked around him and finally stopped, again facing him.

And punched him hard in the chest. Her fist was small, but she had the power of her girth behind her, for she was a lady of ample proportions, and the blow took the breath right out of Samuel's lungs.

"Samuel Kumalo! I had to make sure that you were not a ghost! For four years you are away at war. Never even one letter, not one single letter to say you are alive and well. Not one word! How could you be so cruel?"

"Ah, Agnes, you haven't changed!" And Samuel enveloped her in a giant bear-hug and then they were laughing, laughing and crying with happiness and dancing a mindless jig around the old zinc tub.

When they had calmed down a little, Agnes led him into the house. It was past noon now, the day was hot and

Samuel had not forgotten Agnes' prowess at brewing beer. A pint or two of her famous brew would be exactly what the doctor ordered, thought Samuel.

It was dark in the house, but after his eyes had adjusted he saw an elderly woman sitting on a plain wooden chair in the eating area. Samuel recognized her as Agnes' mother. The woman held a sleeping child in her arms. He greeted the old lady with great respect. Your elders, even Shona elders, must always be treated as though they are your own parents. As he greeted the older lady, Samuel clapped his hands together softly, in the traditional way.

Agnes reached towards her mother and lifted up the child, who whimpered once and then awoke, smiling as it saw its mother. She handed the child to Samuel.

"Samuel, please meet Shadreck. He is your son."

"What? My son? How can this be possible?" The surprise on Samuel's face was obvious.

"Au, Samuel, how could you forget? Remember that last time we spent together? Your boss was in the hospital with the wounded hand from the German bullet in Caprivi and you came out here from Umtali. Three days later the two of you had left for overseas and I thought I would never see you again. Shadreck is now over three years old. And yes, I was tempted many times by the men who come to buy my beer, but never once did I succumb. He is *yours*, Samuel."

Samuel lifted the child up and looked at him more closely, turning him this way and that in the muted light from a curtained window. The boy certainly had many features which identified him as a true Kumalo. He looked straight into Samuel's face, exhibiting no fear of this strange big man.

"Hau! He is a strong boy. He will be a great warrior one day. But not with a name like Shadreck. Where on God's earth did you get that name from, Agnes?"

"It was the name of my father's late brother. He also worked in the mine. He died four years ago in a rock-fall."

"He is *my* son," said Samuel with conviction, "and I alone have the right to name him. I wish him to be called Hastings. From this day forth, his name shall be Hastings."

And Agnes merely nodded her head. She knew better than to argue with a prince of the Matabele Royal Family. She, too, remembered the fair-haired Englishman and the bond that had developed between him and Samuel, a bond only strengthened by Samuel's bludgeoning of a German officer at Schuckmannsburg. Samuel himself had told her the story, not in any boastful way, of how the German had had a Luger in his hand and an evil look in his eye as he squinted down the barrel so intent on taking Hastings' life. The Luger bullet had shattered Hastings' protective, outstretched hand just a moment before Samuel's Mopani-wood *knobkerrie* had spattered the man's head like an over-ripe watermelon and dispatched the German to his very own Valhalla.

Chapter 3

Rezende Mine, Penhalonga, December, 1918

There are some things which seem to occur only in Africa and which are incapable of explanation. Can one reasonably explain, for example, how word of Samuel's arrival at Agnes' father's house could have been communicated within one hour to a certain administrative assistant located two miles away at the mine offices? There had been no drums pounding out an arcane and cryptic message; no young man sent on a bicycle, pedalling swiftly to bear the news; no hard-panting runner arriving with a heaving chest, bearing a scrap of paper. No, none of these. It seemed that the news arrived on the whispering breeze, or perhaps on the warm thermals upon which eagles soar in their high patrols. One minute Tambaguta was busy in the clerical office working busily on the weekly payroll, the next he was knocking on Eddie Evan's office door saying, "*Ishe,* Samuel Kumalo has returned from the war. He is at Amos' house, down at the mine compound."

And Eddie had never thought to question how Tambaguta had come by this information. For Eddie was also an

African, albeit a white African, and he *just knew*. Knew that these things happened. Inexplicably.

The news of Samuel's arrival brought forth a rush of emotions in Eddie. He and his wife, Bella, now expecting their second child, had been devastated when they received the letter from Hastings' wife Tina in Paris giving the news of Hastings' tragic death by German anti-aircraft fire. They had both been so close to Hastings, like a brother, nay, closer, if that could be possible. They had kept his letters, including that final, fateful one clearly marked *To be opened only in the event of my death.* They had sealed the letters up in the Wedgwood biscuit barrel that Hastings had given them on their wedding day in July 1914. So disturbing were the contents of that final, fateful letter, that Eddie had soldered the lid tight-shut.

Eddie thought back on all that had transpired in the intervening four years since he had last seen Hastings and Samuel. For sure the Rezende Mine had grown apace, the yields were better now, the old four stamp mill replaced by a ball-mill which operated so much more efficiently. He had purchased a second mine, too, the Revue, from a war-widow, and also owned a half interest in a third.

He smiled when he remembered how he had first met Trooper Hastings Follett and Constable Samuel Kumalo. It had all been because of a gold thief whom he had apprehended in the very act of stealing gold amalgam from his safe. He and Tambaguta had taken the man, Justice Sibanda was his name, and locked him up in an unused steel boiler to keep him safe overnight until the police could arrive to take him away to Umtali. But Sibanda had

been dead the next morning. The cause of death had been asphyxiation they suspected, and Eddie had fully expected to be trundled off for at least a one year prison term as a guest of His majesty, King George the Fifth.
Manslaughter, even when accidental, was not taken lightly in Rhodesia.

And then Hastings and Samuel had quickly proved it was not a tragic accident but a murder. A well-planned murder to cover up the fact that Sibanda was but a small link in a very large gold stealing operation. Oh yes, he owed those two a lot.

"Tambaguta!"

"*Ishe?*"

"I want to see Constable Kumalo as soon as he is free." Eddie looked at his watch. "Ask him to join me for afternoon tea at, say, three o'clock. And see if we have any of those Marie Biscuits left."

§

That afternoon the two men grasped each others' arms as brothers do, for they shared a common love and a common grief, the death of their friend Hastings Follett. They drank their tea in companionable conversation, the sweet condensed milk cloying on their tongues, and taking small bites out of flat round Marie biscuits. Samuel told Eddie all that had happened in France before he had left to fight in East Africa. And Eddie shared with Samuel the last letters he had received from Hastings, the ones that spoke of his love of flying, and his love for a French singer whom he had met in a nightclub in Paris and of the daughter that had been born a month after his death. But he never shared the contents of that final letter from Hastings. The one that gave such detail of what had happened in the last forty-eight hours before Hastings and Samuel had departed on the troop train for Beira and later the troopship bound for France. That last letter was a confession. And like a priest in his confessional, he could never tell Samuel what message that letter contained. He had sealed it, soldered it into Hastings' wedding present to him and Bella, the Wedgwood biscuit barrel, hopefully never again to see the light of day. No! Samuel must only remember Hastings as a good and honorable man, the man who had so thoroughly dealt with Frikkie Meyer the child molester, not the man who had so coldly put a bullet in Colonel Vlok's arrogant, aristocratic, sabre-scarred Austrian head.

And then they talked of Samuel's time in East Africa, of the cleverness and zeal of the German Colonel von Lettow-Vorbeck. Of the South African general, Jannie Smuts and his successor, Jaap Van Deventer. Of the heat, the rain and the thirst. Of how the King's African Rifles had performed so very well in such very difficult circumstances, led by mostly inept officers.

"So, Samuel," said Eddie, "you're back, you're healthy, unwounded, what now? Back to being a policeman?"

"Yes, sir, I love police work. But I have a problem. I want to stay here in Manicaland. There is someone whom I wish to marry here in Penhalonga. But PGHQ are talking of posting me to either Mashonaland or Matabeleland. So I'm sure you can see my dilemma."

"But you *are* a Matabele, aren't you? I'm sure Hastings told me that your grandfather was King Lobengula."

"It is true. But I will soon have a wife from these parts, and I have a son, too, so I want to stay here. And besides, I am only a third son of a fifth son of a junior wife, so I will not be so readily welcomed back in Matabeleland. No, here is where I want to be."

"You know, Samuel, if you would even consider it, I may have a job for you."

Samuel's eyebrows shot up with immediate interest.

"I am not a miner, sir. I really don't like dark places very much," he said dubiously.

Eddie laughed. "No, no, nothing like that. I need to set up a security department, nothing big or fancy, mind, maybe just two or three people whom I can trust implicitly."

Samuel was nodding his head.

"It's the gold, you see, Samuel. Despite catching that thief Sibanda, I am certain I am still losing product. My operating margins are just too thin to bear the loss of any gold, even one ounce. What do you think, Samuel? Head of Security for Evans Consolidated Gold Mines? Twenty pounds a month, plus a company house. And, what is more, the company is still growing, so this could become a big job with time."

"I will be in charge? You trust me to run your security?"

"No question about it."

For Samuel who remembered so clearly the insult of his demobilization papers, there was not a lot of thought to be given to his decision. He held out his hand.

"I accept, sir, on one condition: I need a motor-cycle for the job."

§

On January 1, 1919, having been helped by Eddie to compose a very polite letter of resignation to PGHQ in Salisbury (no sense in burning bridges), Samuel Kumalo became the first, and for many years, the only, head of security for Evans Consolidated Mines. Oh, and he had the sole and unfettered use of a war surplus, but virtually new, twin cylinder, 425cc, Royal Enfield motorcycle. No, it wasn't an Indian, and it was a real bitch to start, but it would do.

Chapter 4

The protocol for marrying a Shona girl is a thing of great complexity. It is very important for the future success of the marriage that all steps in the procedure, known as *roora,* be undertaken correctly and with great delicacy. At its very heart, a Shona marriage is a business venture, with middle-men (well, actually, more likely middle-women), and far-ranging price negotiations for a number of different items related to the marriage, and so forth.

In Samuel and Agnes' case the protocol was complicated by the fact that Agnes had already borne a child by the prospective husband. Since Samuel had acknowledged that the boy was his, it had been necessary to agree to pay compensation to Agnes' father. A child born out of wedlock is no small thing in Shona society. It was agreed after much haggling, that compensation would amount to one heifer. Then there was the question of *rusambo,* or bride-price. Agnes had completed a standard two education at the Anglican mission school in the Honde Valley, and her father considered this level of education to be akin to a university degree, which, compared to his own formal education, it probably was. In Shona culture, the higher the education level attained by the bride, the greater the *rusambo*.

Agnes' father's go-between, a heavily wrinkled lady of great age named Maria-*mdiki*, literally translated as Little Maria, although she was by no means little, demanded that Samuel deliver ten cattle. To soften the blow, she agreed to take five now, of which one must be a bull of proven fertility, and a further five at a rate of one per year for five years commencing on the first anniversary of the marriage.

Samuel thought that this demand was a little steep, but then justified the price in his mind, not on the basis of Agnes' higher education, but rather on her extraordinary ability to brew *doro*. This talent would be worth its weight in gold in the future. After all, reasoned the groom, there were almost three hundred men living in the labour compound of the Rezende Mine, their thirst greatly magnified by the heavy labour they performed in the hot and humid depths of the underground workings. If she managed the enterprise correctly, Agnes and her future husband could soon be quite comfortable, if not wealthy.

In lieu of actual cattle, of which, as we have seen, Samuel had agreed to deliver a total of eleven, Amos Nyatoti, his future father-in-law, had consented to take half in cash, in advance. At an agreed fair market price of two pounds per head, this amounted to a grand total of eleven pounds owed by Samuel. Once the initial payment was made, the wedding celebrations could finally begin.

In Shona culture, a wedding is a terrific excuse to eat to excess, and drink *doro* until your belly is as tight as the skin of one of the many drums, the *ngoma,* that start beating as soon as the ceremony is over.

Samuel was not at all religious in the western sense of the word, but his bride, by virtue of her mission education, considered herself to be nominally Anglican. She had asked for a religious man to perform the ceremony.

There was an Anglican church in Penhalonga now, housed in a small building on the unpaved main street of the village. Eddie, Bella and some of their friends had put up the money to build the church, but the congregation was still too small to justify a permanent pastor. Graham Parsons D.D, drove out from Umtali every second Sunday, and it was he who, for a small fee, had agreed to come out to formalise the union between Samuel Kumalo, bachelor, of Lupane, Matabeleland, and Agnes Nyatoti, spinster, daughter of Amos Nyatoti of Penhalonga, Manicaland.

§

And what a wedding it was!

Two of Samuel's brothers had travelled out from Gwanda, a small mining town south of Bulawayo, where they worked on a gold mine. Samuel's father, a commander of one of King Lobengula's regiments, had died in the Matabele War of 1893 when Samuel was but a babe in arms. The Induna had been killed instantly on the banks of the Bembezi River by a bullet from a chattering British Maxim machine gun. Samuel's mother was still alive, although now too old to travel, and she had sent some money with Samuel's brothers to buy a fattened ox for the wedding feast. This gesture was very much appreciated by Agnes' father. He had fully expected to take the entire wedding expense on his own shoulders.

Eddie, Bella and little Dorrie, a toddler of two, were there as well as Superintendent Thorneycroft and his wife Elspeth. Mrs.Pennefather, a widow for some three years now, and who still lived on her 15 acre smallholding on the outskirts of town, had volunteered to make Agnes' wedding gown. It was a simple affair of white taffeta complemented by white satin shoes from an Umtali shoemaker. These Samuel had bought for her on one of his periodic trips into the big town. They were the first pair of shoes Agnes had ever owned.

Eddie had insisted on shutting the mine for a full shift so that as many people as possible from the work-force could attend the wedding feast. This had been a risky decision on his part, for with the vast quantities of *doro* likely to be consumed at the wedding he had no guarantee when or even if, the workers would return to their duties.

From the size of the crowd, it seemed that no-one had declined the open invitation. In the days before the wedding, Agnes had brewed six forty-four gallon barrels of beer and had spiked it with some potent *skokiaan* spirit from heaven knew where. There were also circulating surreptitiously quite a number of bottles of *kachasu,* a very potent distilled spirit made with the fruit of the *masao* berry. Samuel knew from his policing days that the spirit was not brewed in Manicaland because the *masao* tree prefers a drier climate, such as that up in the northeast of the country around Mount Darwin and up beyond Dotito on the way to Mukumbura. The *Makorekore* people who inhabit that area are expert at brewing and distilling *kachasu*, know well the secrets of the *masao* berry. Know that it must not be picked straight off the tree or the fruit will not ferment. Know that it must be gathered on the same day it has fallen from the tree, because any later and the *kachasu* will taste bitter. Know that the first distillation gives a liquor that looks remarkably like urine and doesn't taste much better. Know that the second distillation provides a liquor the colour of lemons, palatable, but not commanding a good price. But know that the third distillation gives a liquor as clear as water from the Mazoe River as it tumbles over the high escarpment on its way to the mighty Zambezi. And above all, know not to drink this third distillation to excess, for blindness can often be the unfortunate result.

After the marriage ceremony, which in the late January heat was mercifully short, there were only three speeches. Amos, as father of the bride, with words that were simple but well enunciated, welcomed all the guests. Eddie, fluent in both *IsiNdebele* and *Chishona* made a toast to the newly-married couple. He likened the union as one between a prince and a princess, praising Samuel for his bravery in battle, and for saving the life of his friend, Hastings Follett. The final speech was made by Spencer Thorneycroft as Samuel's immediate predecessor employer. He referred to Samuel's close relationship with the late Hastings Follett, the successes they had had together in solving some pretty vicious murders, and how pleased Trooper Follett would have been with this union.

And then the children from Bella's one-room school began to sing a simple little song of happiness. As they came to the chorus, the entire workforce burst into song in three and four part harmony. Angels in their heaven could not have provided a better choir.

§

Samuel and Agnes mingled with all the guests, and each one pressed a little gift into his or her palm. It might be a silver crown or a five or ten shilling note, but whatever it was, it was given with affection and happiness for the bride and groom, for they were both well-loved in the community, despite Samuel being a Matabele. It had been less than thirty years since the arrival of Rhodes and his white settlers had put a stop to Matabele raiding parties, and memories ran deep.

There was one old lady, however, who seemed very sad. Samuel had even noticed her crying at certain points in the ceremony. Towards the end of the reception, as the crowd began to dwindle and stagger off to their various abodes, he turned to Agnes and asked, "Agnes, why is that mother over there so sad?" and he pointed with his chin to the old lady who sat all alone.

"She recently lost her only son," Agnes answered, "he was buried just three days ago."

"Hau, that is sad. Had he been ill? Was it Spanish Flu?" A particularly virulent strain of flu had appeared towards the end of the war, initially in Europe, but now in Africa as well, and it was a killer. In some parts of Rhodesia up to forty percent of people who contracted the flu did not survive.

"No, they say he was killed by a warthog."

"What! A warthog!?" Samuel was incredulous. He had heard of many different ways of being killed in the bush; indeed, as a young herd-boy near Lupane in northern Matabeleland, he had seen one of his friend's dead body after having been mauled by a lion. It wasn't very pretty. Leopards, elephants, rhinos and Cape buffalo, all of these, yes, even a snake, but death by a warthog? That seemed very unusual.

"Where did this happen?" Samuel asked

"They found his body at the Old Umtali Methodist Mission, the one near the turn-off to new Umtali. He was a teacher at the school there."

"Hmmmm," muttered Samuel, his mind churning. None of what he had heard seemed to make any sense.

No sense at all.

Chapter 5

Eddie Evans was smiling. "Good morning, Samuel."

And it *was* a good morning for Eddie Evans. Despite his fears and misgivings, there had been only three absentees that morning, notwithstanding the extraordinary volume of beer that had been consumed at Samuel and Agnes' wedding the previous Saturday evening. And Samuel looked as though he was very pleased with himself as well.

"*Sakuona, Inkosi,*" he greeted Eddie, who was in his office going through the production reports of the previous week. "May I have a word, sir?"

"Of course. Come in, sit down. How's your new house?"

In his position as security chief, Samuel qualified for one of the few brick and iron cottages in the mine village, and it was to this that Eddie was referring.

"Oh, it is very nice, sir, thank you. Agnes is an excellent house-maker. It will take a few days to get properly settled in, but I am sure we will be very happy there. We need to get a few more pieces of furniture, but there is no hurry for that."

"Good, good. Samuel, thanks again for inviting me and the missus to your wedding. It was a wonderful event. The singing was incredible."

"You are welcome, sir. I agree, these Shona people really know how to sing. Everything went so well, and there were no fights, everyone so happy."

"Yes, and I'm glad to say, we only had three no-shows at shift-start this morning. There were a few of the men that I thought might be nursing terrific hangovers and were wobbly on their feet, but overall, not bad, all things considered. Now, I take it you came to see me for a purpose? What's on your mind?"

"There was one potential benefit from the party. As the men got drunker, I overheard one of them talking about a gold-stealing gang who are working both here and at the Revue Mine."

At the mention of Eddie's second mine, his eyebrows shot up. "What, the Revue too? I mean, I can tell that there is something going on here at Rezende. Actual production just doesn't match the drill assays, even allowing for some wastage. But the Revue? Results there seem to be much closer to what we would expect." At this, Eddie shuffled some papers and handed Samuel the Revue production sheet for the week ended the previous Friday.

"See? Here and here?" His nicotine-stained index finger pointed to drill assays for the area being mined versus actual results. The two numbers were within four percent of each other.

Samuel was nodding his head as he looked at the numbers. "Maybe the drill assays are wrong? Could they be too low?"

"Hmmm. Yes, that could be. The drilling was done before I took over the Revue so I can't vouch for its accuracy. You may have a point." Eddie looked up from the spread-sheets. "So what do you think should be done?"

"I would like to go underground for a few days, literally underground. No-one knows me at the Revue Mine, but I think I know who the gold thieves are, or at least the ring-leaders. But I need to know how they are doing it, because I don't think you are losing amalgam, the security is too tight for that. No, I suspect they are taking actual ore – picking the best pieces of visible gold from the seam and treating it off the mine-site."

Eddie was nodding agreement. "Go," he said, "get to the bottom of this."

"One other thing, sir. I also need to look into something else not connected to the mine."

"Oh yes? What's that?"

"Well, it may be nothing at all, but there was a death last week at Old Umtali mission – a young man, son of a lady who was at our wedding. They say he was gored by a warthog."

"And so? Why should this concern you?"

"It's just that it seems such an unusual way to die. I've never heard of it before. I want to go and have a chat with Doctor Snelgar in Umtali, hear what he has to say. I hope you don't mind me doing this?"

Eddie knew the Medical Examiner for the Umtali district quite well and respected his work.

"No, not at all, you go ahead, Samuel. It sounds very interesting. Just keep me in the loop. Especially concerning the Revue. I'll phone through to the manager there and tell him you'll be working underground for a while."

"No, sir, please do not phone! Let them take me on as a new labourer, on my own strengths. You see, we don't yet know who the members of that gang of thieves are. Your phoning ahead might just tip them off."

"You're absolutely right, Samuel. So fair enough, I'll just wait to hear from you then."

§

The Revue mine was located about fifteen miles from the Rezende, on the road north to Inyanga. When Eddie bought it in 1916, the mine was well managed, but so obviously short of capital. The owner, a young man newly arrived from South Africa, had considered it his patriotic duty to volunteer for service in His Majesty's forces. Thomas Henry Skinner had attested into the 3rd South African Infantry Regiment in early 1915. He had been sent to England to train and was one of the first casualties of the great battle of Delville Wood in western France. He had survived a terrible gaping wound, a machine gun bullet having ripped through his upper thigh. He had been patched up in the field by a regimental surgeon, but had not survived the typhoid which he contracted later. His young widow, Olive, was not yet twenty-two. She had no idea what to do with a small, unprofitable gold mine, and, struggling financially with a mountain of debt, had been only too pleased to accept Eddie's fair offer for the mine. In December 1916, the mine officially changed hands, with a company, Evans Consolidated Mines (Private) Limited, having been set up specifically for the purpose. Six months later, having bought out a minority shareholder in the Rezende, ownership of that mine was also transferred to ECM.

One of the first things that Eddie did when he took over the Revue was to replace its out-dated and inefficient two-stamp mill with the now-idle four-stamp mill from the Rezende. Thus it was that Eddie was able to double milling throughput at both mines within a few months of purchasing the Revue.

§

"Yes? *Unodei?*"

Samuel seethed internally. This labour manager is downright rude, he thought. To come out straight and ask me what I want, as though I were a common peasant. But he sucked it in and kept his thoughts to himself.

"I am looking for work."

"Any mining experience?"

"Four years at the Simmer & Jack in Jo'burg. Blasting, mucking and mill-room labourer." Samuel was parroting the phrases that Eddie had so painstakingly taught him.

"Hmm." Mention of the Simmer & Jack mine in Johannesburg had certainly got the man's attention. Most of the Revue's labour force was comprised of raw young boys from the Tete district in Mozambique or from further north in Nyasaland. Very few had any mining experience at all when they first signed on.

"Well, we may have something available. I need to check with the mine manager. Wait here." The labour man ambled off into one of the offices. Samuel looked around.

The mine appeared to be clean and efficient, with very few idle bodies to be seen. The four-stamp mill was clanking away noisily at one end of the mine, while coco-pans kept trundling out of the mine portal at regular intervals. Samuel could see the laboratory where the gold amalgam was treated and the final product poured into bars. The tall stack adjacent to this building was smokeless today, but Samuel knew that only the biggest mines did a clean-up on a daily basis.

"*Iwe.*" You! Again Samuel seethed at the rudeness of this man, but held his tongue. The labour manager held out several forms secured to a wooden board by a large silver clip. "Fill these in. If you can't write, I will get someone to help you."

Samuel waved his hand dismissively and began filling in the forms using a pencil that was secured to the wooden clipboard with a piece of brown twine. As he wrote, he couldn't help hoping that no-one would find the Royal Enfield hidden in a dry *donga* a few hundred yards from the mine entrance. He had covered it with brush. It should be fine, he thought, but you never can tell with the herd boys these days. They are so inquisitive.

§

Later, Samuel was taken to the single men's barracks in the mine compound, and allocated a narrow bed with a lumpy mattress, two old and well-worn grey blankets and a thin pillow as well as a sturdy metal locker in which to store his few items of clothing. The pay wasn't bad, he thought, one pound per fifty-hour week, but with food, clothing and accommodation included. He couldn't help thinking that Agnes should investigate setting up a second brewery here at the Revue. One hundred and forty men, all far from home and with one pound a week of free money. Hau! What a business!

Next he went to the mine dry to get kitted out with overalls, boots, a metal helmet and an acetylene lamp. The man in charge of the dry told Samuel that his first shift would be at seven the next morning, and not to be late! He had the rest of the day free.

Samuel wandered casually around the mine-site. For a mine that was only in its fourth year of operation a significant amount of old equipment seemed to have accumulated in the 'bone-yard', and it was to this pile of rusting metal that Samuel was attracted. He loved looking at old pieces of machinery and wondering what they had been used for in their past existences. The previous life of the old two-stamp mill was fairly obvious. Unlike the other old machinery, which had become overgrown with creepers and long grass growing wild, the area around the old stamp-mill was clean, the ground free of any growth whatsoever. Samuel's mind was churning as he walked all around the massive, solid steel structure. And as he navigated the rough ground he almost fell, tripped up by a black pipe snaking back into the workings of the boiler plant. He followed the pipe back to its origin, a hole in the boiler room wall. It was in this building that steam was produced for all the large equipment used on the mine property, but mainly for the four stamp mill, the very heart of the mining operation. The black pipe snaked through the hole in the brick wall, but right there at the wall was a steam tap, set in the 'closed' position. Samuel felt it. Hot as Hades. He spat on his hand and then opened the cock slightly. There was a sibilant hiss as steam made its way into the pipe and then suddenly the old two-stamp mill behind him started to clank and he quickly shut down the steam supply with a deft turn of the cock back to the 'closed' position. He hoped no-one had heard the clank as the old mill's flywheel started turning, but the few workers who were around seemed oblivious to the new noise. The ongoing and overpowering cacophony of the rest of the mill operations was just too great.

§

Samuel was up at six the next morning, and along with seventy other miners, attending to his ablutions. There was a separate block with showers and basins, while yet another building held a battery of 'long-drop' toilets. The showers even had a hot-water supply, utilising excess water from the condensers in the boiler room.

He walked out into the sunshine of a cloudless January day. It was going to be a warm one, he thought, and sniffing the air, Samuel suspected there could well be a thunder-storm that afternoon. Still, he didn't care; he'd be underground mucking out the stopes or man-handling coco-pans through the galleries. And he'd be well fed; he could smell that unmistakable aroma of bacon sizzling in the cookhouse.

§

"You! New boy! Come here."

Samuel trotted over to the dry – change-rooms - where his shift was getting ready to go underground.

"I am Boss Godfrey, the shift boss," and a grey-haired, grizzled old white man stuck out his hand. Samuel studied him carefully. This was the person into whose hands he would be delivering his very life for the next ten hours. Godfrey had once been tall, but a lifetime of hard work and an accident or two had put a kink in his back. One of his knees was bowed to an extraordinary degree, and as Samuel took the proffered hand, he could sense that Godfrey had lost a finger or two as well.

"You're Samuel, hey? They told me you worked at Simmer & Jack? I was at Village Main Reef for twenty years. Busted my back and knee in a pressure-burst on five-level back in 1908. They didn't want me after that, so here I am in sunny Rhodesia!" And he slapped his good knee. "I may have a crock back but I can still outwork any one of you darkies!"

Samuel smiled. He was a rough old geezer, but he believed that his heart was in the right place. What's more, he thought, he knows gold-mining. No green-horn this one. And with his old injuries he would probably be reluctant to put his crew in harm's way.

Samuel was the only one on the shift who didn't have a lunch-box. He had taken a sandwich from the mess-hall where they had had breakfast. He had put it in one of the large pockets in his mine-issued overalls, along with an orange.

They used empty coco-pans to ride into the mine. The narrow-gauge rail system used for hauling the ore out of the mine extended almost to the working face itself.

The work he was put to was hard but somehow satisfying. Samuel's crew had the task of mucking out the faces where blasting had taken place at the end of the previous shift. The drilling and setting of explosives had been performed by the crew before them, and now all that was left was to clean up the various working faces, load the coco-pans with ore, then send the conveyances away to the mill. Samuel could feel his hands beginning to become a little raw. Apart from chasing Germans in East Africa he had not done much physical work over the past two years. After all, a Regimental Sergeant Major does not stoop to manual labour!

From what he could see by the light of his acetylene lamp, the ore in this particular area of the mine was rich, a pure white quartz run through with fine strings of gold. They were working a seam that appeared to be four feet wide and laced through with visible gold. Samuel made a mental note to suggest that Eddie do some supplemental core drilling inside the mine and assay the results.

At noon Mr. Godfrey called for a lunch break. They had been working for a solid five hours and Samuel needed a break. His stomach was growling loudly. He and the rest of the crew sat in little groups of four or five men and talked of their homes and their loved ones so far away.

After they had finished their lunches the men picked up their shovels, and with their lunch boxes in hand, headed back to work.

§

At the end of their shift, all of them sweating profusely and grimy with dust, the miners trudged out of the mine. One of the men walking alongside Samuel stopped at a cross-cut to relieve himself and laid down his lunch-box so as to free his hands for a more important, delicate, task. As the man disappeared into the dark cross-cut, on a hunch, Samuel leaned down and picked up the man's lunch-box by its handle. The small metal box must have weighed over twenty pounds.

Chapter 6

It was dark when Samuel reached the shallow ravine or
donga where he had hidden his Royal Enfield. At first he
couldn't find it, and became anxious, but then by the light
of a quarter-moon he saw a glint of glass and chrome under
dried leaves and started the long, careful process of
removing the thorny brush he had piled atop the machine.
He wheeled the motor-cycle back onto the Penhalonga road
then fired it up. It fired first kick, quite unusual for a Royal
Enfield, but when he came to turn on the headlamp, he
couldn't find the switch. And then it suddenly dawned on
him that, being a war-surplus machine, the light switch may
well have been removed for security reasons.

He rode the fifteen miles to the Rezende in complete and
utter darkness, literally crawling along and feeling his way
along the rutted, corrugated road. The quarter-moon was of
no help whatsoever. It took almost an hour, but he arrived
without mishap or incident, then rode down to his house to
report in to his real boss – Agnes.

She greeted her new husband with much love and affection
and, best of all, with a large blue enamel mug of her best
doro. She made him sit down at the kitchen table, then
brought Hastings through for Samuel to hold. As he played

with his son, who chatted away in that unselfconscious way that all three year olds do, Samuel wondered at this amazing product of his and Agnes' love. He was a big boy for his age, with bright, intelligent eyes, and an uncanny ability to complete jigsaw puzzles in almost no time at all. Bella Evans had recommended that Agnes enrol him in school at age five rather than six, because she felt the child had a special intelligence that needed to be nurtured and developed. And Bella should know. She was the only school-teacher for miles around.

After he had eaten the *sadza* and stew that Agnes put in front of him, Samuel told Agnes that he had to go out for a little while. In answer to her enquiring look he said simply, "Business."

§

It was Bella who answered Samuel's knock at the Evans' front door. Samuel remembered the house so well. It was the same one that Eddie had lived in as a bachelor when Samuel and Hastings had first arrived in Penhalonga nearly five years earlier. Still the same pots of red geraniums lining the front of the verandah.

"Samuel," she said, "what a nice surprise." She turned towards the interior of the house. "Eddie!" she called out, "Samuel is here to see you. Please, Samuel, come in, come in." And she opened the door wide to admit the big man.

Eddie came through in his dressing gown and slippers and Samuel suddenly felt that he was intruding, that whatever he had to say could easily have waited until tomorrow. But then he saw the glass of whisky in Eddie's hand and changed his mind about getting up and leaving.

Eddie took him into the living room and, after refusing an offer of beer or whiskey, Samuel brought him up to date on everything he had seen at the Revue mine, and how he thought gold was being stolen.

"Sir, I think that if you do some infill drilling you might just find that your grades at Revue are much better than you thought. The ore I saw was beautiful, with visible gold in almost every chunk. The mucking crew are selecting the best samples they come across during their shift and taking them out in their lunch-boxes."

"You're joking! Their lunch-boxes, hey? The buggers! Do you think Godfrey's in on it?"

"My instinct tells me no, but if a complete rookie like me could see what they were doing, why is Godfrey missing it?"

"But Samuel, stealing ore is all well and good, but how are they processing it? It still has to be crushed and milled and the gold extracted."

"That was what I discovered first, yesterday, when I arrived at the mine. I think they are using the old two-stamp mill to grind the ore. It's in the bone-yard and still connected to the steam supply from the boiler."

"What? No, I just can't believe it!" Eddie seemed incredulous. "This is worse than I thought. The mine manager *must* be in on it. How could such a sophisticated operation go on without his knowledge? It was just as well you stopped me from phoning ahead and warning him of your arrival. So what do we do now, Mr. Chief of Security?"

"Leave it to me, sir," said Samuel. He got up and said goodbye to Bella who was in the bedroom brushing her daughter Dorrie's thick blonde hair.

A moment later they heard the low guttural roar of a two cylinder motor-cycle fire up and head back down the road towards the mine. Eddie stood at the bedroom doorway looking on at Bella's nightly hairdressing activities. "That Samuel Kumalo," he said, "is one hell of a smart cookie."

§

Christmas Pass is the name the early European settlers in Umtali gave to the route through the mountains that surround the city. The town itself sits in an amphitheatre-like arrowhead-shaped bowl surrounded by mountains, open only to the east. The railway line takes this open route through the border-post at Machipanda onwards to the port of Beira and the deep blue waters of the Indian Ocean.

On this day Christmas Pass was shrouded in mist, cold and wet, and Samuel began to regret his decision to visit the Umtali Police Post and his old boss Spencer Thorneycroft. But he couldn't back out now, despite the weather. He had phoned ahead from the mine where he now had his own office, and Thorneycroft was expecting him. Samuel had been vague on the agenda for their meeting, saying only that it was a 'criminal matter'.

The gravel road down into Umtali from atop Christmas Pass was treacherous for a motor-cycle, and Samuel almost lost control on a couple of occasions, his back wheel slipping and sliding in the viscous mud. He was wearing a rubberized poncho, part of his army kit issue which had somehow not found its way back into central stores. Every soldier that ever there was has something in his possession that 'somehow' fails to be returned after a war. Nonetheless, by the time he knocked on Thorneycroft's office door he was feeling very self-conscious about his mud-spattered clothes.

The *guti* or misty weather they were now experiencing was not unusual for Umtali, but the policeman seated in front of Samuel would clearly never get used to it. This was the kind of weather in which his Boer War leg wound really began to bother him. A Boer sniper armed with a Mauser rifle had put a dum-dum bullet in his right leg back in 1901. He was lucky not to have lost the limb, for the damage that that particular bullet can do to human flesh is beyond imagining. It had been Doc Snelgar who had saved the leg, and now, eighteen years later, here were the two of them working closely together in Umtali, Thorneycroft as CO of British South Africa Police, Manicaland Province and Snelgar as the Chief Medical Officer. In this kind of weather, all Thorneycroft could do was to rub the old wound incessantly.

"Well, Samuel, what can I do for you today?" The man was obviously not in the mood for idle chit-chat. Not even a word about how much he had enjoyed the wedding. Of course it had been sunny that day and his leg hadn't bothered him at all.

"There are two things I wish to discuss, sir. The first has to do with illegal gold dealing."

"Oh, Samuel, not again! This conversation is like *déjà vu*. Wasn't that Sibanda case all about gold theft? Wasn't that Follett's case?"

"You are correct, sir, but that was at the Rezende. This time the thieving is going on at the Revue Mine. I need a little more time to finalise my investigation, but I will need your help to make the necessary arrests and so forth. Now that I am no longer with the police, I am not sure that the magistrate will agree that I have the requisite authority to apprehend the culprits."

"Hmmm, no, probably not. Yes, just as well that you give us the heads-up on this case." He picked up a fountain pen and began writing notes on a pad of lined note paper. "Tell you what, Samuel, I'm going to introduce you to a young trooper whom I will appoint as case liaison officer. His name is Simcoe. Barry Simcoe. Go easy on him, Samuel. He only arrived from Depot about three weeks ago, and before Depot, fresh off the boat from England. He's raw, but he's smart and I think the two of you will get on well together." He paused and cranked the field telephone set that sat on one corner of his desk.

"Operator? Thorneycroft here. Please patch me through to

Trooper Simcoe." There was a short delay then, "Simcoe, yes it is. Please come through to my office right away."

Thorneycroft turned to Samuel. "You said there were two things, Samuel."

"Yes sir. The second issue is a little more nebulous." Thorneycroft was thinking, where in the hell did this chap learn words like nebulous?

"Go on."

"Well, there is this *amai-* mother, who was at the wedding on Saturday." Thorneycroft was nodding his head. "She was very sad, sometimes she was even weeping."

"It's not a crime to be sad, Samuel."

"No sir, please forgive me for not getting to the point. When I enquired what the problem was, I learned that her only son was killed last week."

"Was that the case of the body found at the mission at Old Umtali? Some animal had gored him?" Thorneycroft was renowned for knowing just about everything that went on in his district.

"Yes, sir, that is the very one. The deceased's name was Gideon Munyaradzi, and he was employed at the Methodist mission in Old Umtali. A teacher, a very good one I have been told"

"But I don't understand why you are so concerned. It seems to me to be an open and shut case of an animal attack causing death. It *does* happen from time to time, you know. No crime there."

"I agree, sir, but what concerns me is the type of animal suspected of doing the goring. They say it was a warthog. Now in my experience, warthogs, as ugly and ferocious as they appear to be, are actually very timid animals and will run away squealing at the first sight of a human."

"Go on." Thorneycroft had stopped rubbing his leg. He leaned forward in his chair. He was definitely interested in what Samuel was saying.

"Furthermore, sir, even the largest warthog would not, in my opinion, be capable of goring a fully-grown man, certainly not in the buttocks and groin where I have been told Gideon had been gored."

Thorneycroft was now fully engaged, nodding his head quite vigorously.

"You're abso-bloody-lutely right, Samuel! Now that I think on it, it seems impossible for a warthog to be responsible. Unless."

"Unless what, sir?"

"Unless the victim was lying prone on the ground."

"That is correct, sir, but think about one other thing. A warthog's tusk is too curved to be able to do what it was supposed to have done if the body was lying prone on the ground. The angles are wrong. At least that is what my instinct tells me."

"So what do you want to do here, Samuel?"

Well, sir, with your permission, I would like to make a full investigation, including an exhumation and possibly an autopsy by the Medical Examiner."

Thorneycroft pondered Samuel's request for a moment. Orders for exhumations were not that easy to obtain. Then he nodded his head. "Very well, Samuel, that seems reasonable. We'll leave it that this matter is unofficial at this stage, no formal docket, and that you are conducting an investigation on behalf of the family of the deceased?"

§

Barry Simcoe was a tall, well-built young man of around twenty-two, short blond hair above a ruddy plump face. His blue eyes showed intelligence and his smile betrayed a readiness to please his boss.

"Simcoe, I'd like you to meet one of our more famous former Umtali members, Samuel Kumalo, newly returned from the war in East Africa. He earned a field commendation during the action in Caprivi at the start of the war, and went to France as well. Demobbed as an RSM."

"Kumalo. Nice to meet you." Simcoe stuck his hand out and Samuel was surprised at the strength of his handshake.

"Kumalo resigned from the force at the end of December and has taken a position as security man with Evans Consolidated Mines. They're the company that owns the Rezende and Revue Mines out Penhalonga way. Eddie

Evans is the owner, his wife Bella runs the local primary school."

Simcoe was absorbing this information, nodding his head in understanding.

"One of the things that gold miners have to be really careful of is gold theft, and the administration feels so strongly about it that a law has been passed making illegal gold dealing a very serious crime. It carries a possible five year sentence for a first offence, ten for a second.

"Anyway, Kumalo thinks he's onto a well-organised group of individuals who are getting away with as much as seven to ten ounces a day." He looked at Samuel for confirmation. Samuel nodded his agreement.

"Now Kumalo has no powers of arrest except under very limited circumstances, so he has asked if we will stay close to the case and assist when it comes time to start making arrests. I am tasking you, Simcoe, with being the police liaison on this case. Think you can do it?"

"Absolutely," said Simcoe, nodding his head vigorously. He looked quite excited at the prospect of some field work.

§

Leaving Simcoe to start opening official dockets, Samuel's next port of call was the Umtali General Hospital. He wanted to see Doc Snelgar, the government pathologist who was responsible for autopsies in the region.

As he walked past the nurses' lunchroom he glanced in and saw Elspeth Thorneycroft sitting there having a cup of tea. Samuel remembered so clearly when he had first met Elspeth (she had been single back then), such a shy and retiring nurse, never saying anything or venturing an opinion. And then Superintendent Thorneycroft had asked her to accompany him to the opening of the Penhalonga Police Station in May 1914, and the rest was history. They had married the following year, and she had produced a son a year later, although by then Samuel had been in France. She and her husband had been at Samuel's wedding, although he had not had much time to say more than a quick hello.

"Hello Missus Thorneycroft." She looked up from her magazine.

"Well, hello Samuel, what brings you to the hospital?"

"Oh, nothing much. I just want a quick consultation with old Doc Snelgar. By the way, where is Connie Snyman?"

"She's in Cape Town at the moment. She went down to visit her parents for Christmas. She should be back the beginning of next week. I'll tell her you're back. She'll be sad to have missed you. Be gentle with her when you do see her, Samuel. She is still grieving Hastings' death." She didn't have to say any more. Samuel knew that Connie had held a candle for Hastings from the moment they had first met. Sadly the love was not reciprocated. Hastings had regretted it, but, as he had explained to Samuel over a few beers on board the troopship to France, there had just been 'no chemistry'.

Doc Snelgar was in his evil-smelling examination room, the odour of formalin and stomach contents lying foetid on the air. He was sitting at the same old cigarette-and-coffee-stained wooden desk, plunking away two-fingered on the same old Remington typewriter, a lit cigarette lying forgotten in a stub-strewn glass ashtray, grey smoke curling lethargically to the ceiling. Samuel remembered both the typewriter and the ashtray clearly from four years before. Some things just never change, he thought.

The grizzled old veteran of the Boer War looked up from his work. "Samuel Kumalo!" he said, emphasising each word theatrically. "I had heard you were back in town. Left the police, got a job with Eddie Evans and tied the marriage knot as well. All within a week or two of demobbing from the army! Congratulations old fellow!" and he got up and took Samuel's hand. "So sorry about your friend Hastings," he said, a sad look coming over his lined face. "He was a good chap. I suspect he was destined for greater things than policing."

"Yes, sir, I miss him a lot. Everyone does. You know, I suppose, that he left a wife and baby daughter in France?"

"Yes, Eddie Evans told me all about it. What a shame. Anyway, old chap, I suppose you're here for a purpose and not just to shoot the breeze, as the Americans would say."

"Um, yes, Doctor. I was wondering if you could help me on a professional matter."

"Well, I can't promise anything, but go on, shoot. I hope you didn't pick up a dose of something in East Africa. I've heard that those Kikuyu maidens are very easy with their affections. Does it burn like hell when you pee?"

Samuel laughed, slapping his thigh. "No, nothing like that! I never had time to chase after the Kikuyu girls; we were always too busy chasing after General Vorbeck.
"Look, doctor, there was this young man found dead out at the Old Umtali mission last week. His mother tells me he was gored by a warthog."

"Ah yes, I believe I heard about that. But since his body wasn't sent through here for an autopsy, it's obvious that the powers that be didn't consider there to be any suspicious circumstances surrounding his death."

"And on the surface, sir, they would be right. But *I* am suspicious. I just find it really difficult to believe that a warthog could inflict a wound that could kill a grown man. A child, perhaps, but a grown, adult man? No. This I cannot believe."

"So what are you suggesting?"

"I think the least we can do is to have the body exhumed and for you to do a full autopsy. He has only been in the ground for four days so the body should still be in fairly good condition."

"Samuel Kumalo! Good God, man, do you realise just what is involved in getting a body exhumed? It's not that simple."

"I know, but that is why I came to see *you*. If anyone can do it, Doctor, you can." Praise will often work where all else fails. The doctor went over to a green metal filing cabinet and began looking for the requisite forms. "Aha, here we are. Application for Exhumation. D'you know, Samuel, this is only the second time I've had to fill one of these forms out in the fifteen years I've been in Umtali?"

§

Since Snelgar had told Samuel that obtaining an exhumation order would take quite some time, they had agreed to meet in two hours time outside the main hospital entrance. While he waited for the administration gears to slowly churn down at the Magistrate's office, Samuel had another chore to do. He needed to find out everything there was to know about warthogs.

Not far from the General Hospital, on a quiet, Jacaranda-shaded avenue was a small wooden building. The sign above the verandah read: "Museum of Natural History – Manicaland Branch". Samuel opened the front door with some trepidation. A very studious looking young white man, eyes massively magnified by thick tortoiseshell glasses, sat behind a desk. He stood up and came over when he saw Samuel standing hesitantly at the entrance.

"Come in, come in," he said, a broad smile on his face, "the animals won't bite. My name is Henry Vinson, I'm the curator."

Samuel looked around the building. On every wall was a mounted specimen of almost every animal that it was possible to encounter in the wild. There were the heads of lions, leopards, wildebeest, rhinos, both white and black, with placards showing the differences between the two. One end of the building was taken up by a full-sized stuffed elephant, a pair of magnificent tusks almost touching the floor. Glass cases held other, smaller specimens, but nowhere could Samuel see what he was looking for: *Phacocoerus Africanus*, otherwise known as the common warthog.

"Sir, I wonder if you can help me?" he began, and seeing the eager look on the young man's face, continued, "I was wondering if you have a warthog exhibit."

"That's funny," said Vinson, "you're the second person in a fortnight to ask me the same question. I don't think anyone has asked to see the warthog in a dozen years, and now it's twice in a fortnight. Anyway, no matter, come with me. We keep our *Phacocoerus* in another building. However, I should warn you, we don't have a mounted specimen, only a complete skeleton, I trust that will be OK?"

"Yes, that will be fine," answered Samuel, "I just need to examine its tusks for a project I'm working on."

It was obvious that the outbuilding was rarely visited. It smelt musty, and its glass exhibit cases could have done with a good dusting. Vinson ushered Samuel in to the building, then led him to a large display case. "Here we are," he said, "I'll just leave you to it."

The white bones of a large male warthog were laid out within the case, and it was quite obvious that one of its tusks was missing. The skeleton had only three, two of the almost circular upper tusks, but only one of the fairly

62

straight, but shorter, lower tusks. Samuel opened the hinged glass top quite easily. It was not locked or in any other way secured, and he reached inside and tried to remove the remaining tusks from the skull. It took no effort whatsoever.

Mr. Vinson was seated at his desk when Samuel returned. He looked up, a smile on his face. "Did you find what you wanted?" he asked.

"Yes, thank you very much indeed. I wonder if you can tell me who it was came here two weeks ago to look at the warthog."

"Ah, sorry, didn't catch the young lady's name. An African girl it was. Said she was from the mission over at Old Umtali. A teacher, possibly, but can't be sure. I seem to remember her saying something about a class project."

§

Two hours later Doc Snelgar, Samuel and Barry Simcoe stood at the head of a fresh grave in the Umtali Native Cemetery and watched while two labourers toiled with pick and shovel in a miserable drizzle. Fortunately it was not particularly hard work because the soil in the grave was still soft and friable from the recent burial. In less than half-an- hour, using thick sisal ropes looped around either end, they had hauled the cheap plywood coffin from the depths of Gideon's grave.

The two men loaded the coffin onto the back of the flat-bed Dodge truck that Snelgar had driven to the cemetery, then watched as the truck slowly made its way back onto the

63

main road into town. There would be much discussion about this incident in the native townships that night.

Samuel and Barry wanted to stay and watch Doc Snelgar do his macabre work, but the doc persuaded them to leave, Samuel for home and Barry for the police mess while there was still light. The doctor suggested Samuel phone him before noon the next day for the autopsy results.

Chapter 7

The miserably, cold drizzle of the previous day had given way to bright blue skies and warm sunshine, with nary a cloud to be seen. Samuel was sitting in his small office putting together a plan to present to Eddie. He called it plan 'R' with the 'R' standing for the Revue Mine. It was not going to be easy getting to the bottom of the ore cherry-picking problem. Samuel suspected that the rot at the mine went right to the very top, but it might be very difficult to prove.

He looked at his watch, a gift from Hastings Follett soon after they had arrived in France aboard the SS Pretoria, now more than four long and eventful years ago. Samuel had been given to understand that Hastings had purchased the timepiece from a shady character on the jetty at Port Said when their vessel had berthed there for refueling on its way to Calais. The watch's dubious provenance had not been discussed as Hastings handed over ten shillings, a quarter of what the man had originally demanded. The face was still a brilliant white, with black roman numerals for the hours. Samuel had thought that the hot and steamy jungle fighting in East Africa might have discoloured the face, or affected its workings, but no, the piece still ticked on. And now it said almost noon and hopefully Doc Snelgar would have some information for him. Samuel picked up the black Bakelite phone from its cradle and cranked the metal handle.

"Penhalonga Operator." Samuel recognized the voice as belonging to Gwen Kloppers, wife of Gerhardt Kloppers, a local tobacco farmer. In addition to operating the small telephone exchange, Gwen also ran the post office. The Kloppers family needed the money; tobacco farming was a risky business.

"Ah yes. May I have Umtali General Hospital, please?"

A few minutes after the hospital operator answered, Snelgar's voice came on the line.

"Why do I know that it's you, Kumalo? I said noon and it's only.... oh my God! Is it that time already?"

"Should I call back later, sir?"

"No, no, hang on the line." Samuel could hear Snelgar get up and walk from the wall phone over to his Remington dominated desk. And then he heard his steps coming back.

"Okay, Kumalo, I've completed the autopsy. It's quite remarkable, really, never seen anything like it before. I can tell you first of all that the young man's death can definitely be ruled a homicide. He has a laceration and a fracture to the rear of his skull that hardly bled at all, so I suspect that he died very soon after being clubbed. I can understand why a cursory look may not have revealed that particular wound. From the angle of the lacerations to his buttocks and his groin I would have to agree that they were caused by a sharp object such as a warthog's tusk. However, I suspect that they were incurred while the man was prone, and in and of themselves were not the cause of death."

"So what was the cause of death, then, Doctor? Was it the head wound?"

"No, Samuel, it was poison. No question it was cyanide, I need to do more tests but I'd say it was probably potassium cyanide. Lethal stuff, Kumalo. Doesn't take much to kill a grown man. I need to run some more tests, but I strongly suspect that the poison was introduced through the goring, though where a warthog would get hold of cyanide I couldn't really say." He laughed out loud at his joke.

After Samuel hung up the phone he sat in pensive silence for a few minutes, his head in his hands. He was shocked. Cyanide? He would have to phone Spencer Thorneycroft. This was now a police matter, he would have to stop his investigations. He was no longer a policeman. He had been a fully-fledged civilian for a little less than a fortnight.

§

Doc Snelgar was in Superintendent Spencer Thorneycroft's office at the police camp when Samuel finally got through on the phone.

"Kumalo? Good afternoon. Yes I have just heard. Doc Snelgar is with me right now going though the autopsy. You really *do* have a nose for murders, don't you?" And despite the gravity of the call, they all laughed, Samuel's coming through tinny on the party-line phone.

"So the question is, what to do? We're under the gun here in Umtali; a lot of our young troopers haven't come back from the war in Europe yet. I just don't have the manpower available to get to this case for quite a while. If the magistrate will let me formally deputize you, would you be prepared to continue with the investigation? With Simcoe as your liaison as before?"

"Of course, sir, and on my side I will have to clear it with Mr. Evans."

"Understood. Alright, leave it with me. Doc Snelgar knows the magistrate very well, he has promised to approach him for me."

§

"Underground," answered Tambaguta when Samuel asked him where Eddie Evans was. "Back for lunch at one, he told me." He waved his hand back and forth. "Maybe, maybe not."

Samuel went back into his office. His Plan R needed some refinements.

A few minutes later there was a double-rap on his office door and Samuel looked up.

"I heard you wanted to see me." said Eddie, his face caked with mud and streaked white where the sweat had run from his hair-line. He lit up a Springbok cigarette from a supply that he kept in a chromed cigarette case in the top pocket of his khaki shirt. Samuel had noticed that Eddie smoked a lot more now than he had when he first met him four years ago. He suspected it had something to do with the pressures of the job: running two gold mines was no doubt very stressful.

"Yes, *Inkosi*. Two things we need to talk about. First, I wanted to discuss Revue with you. There are some things that must be done before we make our move on that gang of thieves."

"Yes, Samuel, but you must realise that there are some things which we – you – are not empowered to do. At some point we're going to have to involve the police in this investigation."

"I have already spoken with Superintendent Thorneycroft. He wants me to go ahead with the investigation right up to the point of arrest. He is still short of many key staff, with men still away in Europe. He has appointed a white policeman to be my liaison. His name is Barry Simcoe."

"Oh yes, I know the lad. He only recently arrived from England. He was in my foursome at the golf club on Saturday. Nice enough chap. A little wet behind the ears."

Samuel was nodding his head in agreement.

"Anyway, well done, Samuel, you seem to have covered every administrative contingency. And what's the second thing?"

"I've just received the autopsy results on that young teacher who was supposedly gored by a warthog over at Old Umtali Mission. You know, sir, the one whose mother lives here at the mine?" Eddie was nodding his head. "We obtained permission to exhume his body."

"Go on."

"Doc Snelgar says the man was murdered, looks like cyanide crystals."

"What! Good God, man, that's terrible. So this is now a police matter, I take it?"

"Yes, of course, *Inkosi*, but again, because of his acute staff situation, Mr. Thorneycroft is asking the magistrate to temporarily deputise me to conduct the investigation. I told him I needed to discuss the matter with you before agreeing."

"Well, that's a big thumbs-up for you, Samuel. Old Prick Thorneycroft must think quite highly of you to make that kind of decision. And yes, certainly, go ahead and help on the investigation. We'll put your absence down to community involvement."

"Thank you, *Inkosi*, I will do my best."

"Okay, good. So now, what's the plan for Revue?"

"I suspect, *Inkosi*, that the drill-logs you were shown when you did your original due diligence had been altered. The gold values had been decreased, probably to make you less interested in buying the property. Did you inherit the mine manager?"

"Yes, Blackie Schwartz came with the property. I didn't know him very well, but the late owner's wife, Olive Skinner, vouched for him, said that she trusted him, that he was good with the work-force, and that he kept things going when there was no cash-flow at all. All of that was good enough for me. Yes, I kept him on, and I tell you, Samuel, I'm still not convinced that he's at the root of this."

"That is why you need to spend some money, *Inkosi*. Take a few of the old drill holes, say five or six, and then twin them with new holes." Eddie was nodding his head.

"Twin the holes that are closest to where I was working the other day. If the gold values are the same in both drill logs then Mr. Schwartz is in the clear. If the new holes are higher, as I suspect they will be, then he becomes the person of greatest interest."

"But Samuel, why on earth would he have wanted to alter the drill logs in the first place? Surely he would have wanted higher gold values rather than lower values as you're suggesting?"

"Normally, I would say yes, I agree with you. But not if he himself had wanted to buy the mine from Mrs. Skinner at a fire-sale price."

"But good God, man, Blackie didn't have the kind of money for that. Not back then. No, I think you must be mistaken."

But Samuel could tell from the tone of Eddie's voice that a kernel of doubt had taken root in his boss's brain. Now for the coup-de-grace.

"Would it interest you to know that Mr. Schwartz and Frikkie Meyer are close friends?"

"What!" Eddie was incredulous at the mention of the name of a well-known local ne'er-do-well and pedophile. Maybe Samuel's theory *did* make sense after all. Eddie had known Frikkie's father quite well. A fine upstanding member of the community, he had been a very wealthy farmer in the district. Frikkie was his only son and had inherited everything when the old man died. Oh yes, he would have a few pennies all right. And if Blackie and Frikkie were pals then it was quite reasonable to suspect that the drill logs had been altered such that Eddie would have been disinclined to make the purchase. What the two men hadn't counted on was Eddie's altruism towards the widow of a young man mown down by a German machine gun at Delville Wood in July, 1916. Eddie would probably have bought the mine under any circumstances. As a man whose service had been refused by the army, he felt that it was his patriotic duty to help the poor widow.

He thought back to Blackie Schwartz' demeanour during the due diligence process two years earlier. Now he remembered how reluctant the manager had been in providing information; it had been like pulling teeth.

Nothing was freely volunteered. Eddie felt a cold chill run down his spine. *The bastard has been robbing me blind all this time*, he thought, *and probably the widow and her husband before me. No wonder the couple had always been short of cash and living on their creditors.*

"Inkosi," said Samuel, who had seen the dark look come over Eddie's face, "please don't say anything to anyone until the drilling has confirmed my suspicions one way or the other. And the reason for drilling should be masked by some story or other. Or, better yet, maybe even send Mr. Schwartz away on a well-earned holiday."

§

As it happened, though, Eddie didn't have to send Schwartz away on vacation, although it was quite clear from the attendance record going back some four years that Blackie hadn't missed a single day of work. He was due at least four months worth of holidays. No, in the end, with syrupy grace on the outside and a steely anger on the inside, Eddie had asked his Revue manager to travel to Eddie's third gold mine, the Tafuna in Shamva, a hundred miles away in Mashonaland Province, to do a production audit. Eddie was only a half-owner, but his partner and old Imperial School of Mines pal, Ernie Tupp, had very quickly agreed to the fake audit once Eddie had told him in very strict confidence of his suspicions concerning the Revue mine manager.

Eddie insisted on being at the Revue mine site to supervise the crew from the drilling company. The company did a lot of work for Eddie but the crew captain nonetheless resented

Eddie's presence, perhaps feeling that he was not being trusted to do a good job. Since Eddie was paying the bills, though, he reluctantly accepted him. Eddie was very precise as to where he wanted each drill hole to be sited, having used a theodolite to survey the ground, and was there to collect every core as it came to the surface and was placed in a wooden core box. In the end, after two days of loud clanging of the percussion equipment, they had twinned six of the original drill holes that were located approximately above the area below which Samuel had toiled not many days before. The cores were then placed in long, flat wooden boxes, nailed shut, then sealed and sent off under Samuel's supervision to the assay office in Umtali.

The assayer was not at all happy when Samuel insisted that he be present as each and every one of the six cores was crushed and assayed, but since Eddie had agreed to pay a premium for the rush job, he reluctantly allowed Samuel to remain in the hot and dusty laboratory. Samuel knew a thing or two about 'chain of custody' when it came to evidence. And without question these cores could be considered evidence.

Finally, six hours after his arrival, Samuel was handed a brown envelope with several papers inside.

"These are the assay results. I hope Mr. Evans is satisfied. And please tell him that my invoice is enclosed." With that Samuel drove away in Eddie's flat-bed Model T Ford.

§

It was late in the afternoon when Samuel arrived back at the Revue mine. Eddie was sitting at Blackie Schwartz' desk in the mine manager's office, surrounded by walls plastered with mine plans. Eddie had always left his manager to his own devices, and up until now, had had no complaints. Financial results had always been pretty much bang-on with the budgets and targets set each year by Eddie and his accountants. The return on his investment, though, was much lower than it should have been, and Eddie now knew why.

Eddie couldn't hear the Model T above the clanking of the four-stamp mill, but he could see the plume of dust it was throwing up for several miles before Samuel finally pulled up to the mine offices.

"Well?' asked Eddie, "everything okay?"

Samuel handed over the buff envelope. "It's all in here, boss," he said. "I hope my hunch is right."

Eddie couldn't wait to rip open the envelope, impatiently ushering Samuel before him into the mine office. He sat in silence for a few minutes, studying the assay results. Samuel, looking over his shoulder, could make no sense of the jumble of numbers and symbols that he saw.

After a while Eddie looked up from the papers and said, slowly, almost sadly, "This is far worse than you suspected, Samuel."

"What are we looking at, *Inkosi*? I don't understand these numbers. What do they mean?"

"Okay, Mister Kumalo here beginneth the first lesson." Samuel was a willing student, and, as Eddie already knew, very bright. He was soon busy with a pencil and paper multiplying and dividing the numbers that Eddie gave him from the assay results splayed out on the desk in front of them.

"So, Samuel, the bottom line is that, at a production rate of six tons of ore per shift, three shifts per day, and at an average grade of sixteen pennyweights of gold per ton, which is what the original drill results showed, the mine should have an output of fourteen and a half ounces per day. For the full year of 1917 the mine recorded only 3,500 ounces, versus about 5,500 ounces."

"But when did you swap out the old two stamper for the four stamp mill now in operation?"

"That's one hell of a good question coming from a non-miner! Yes, you're right. We swapped it out in mid-year, 1917 so.." Eddie paused with the eraser-end of a yellow wooden pencil in his mouth. "Hmm, there you are, almost bang on, based on 16 pennyweight ore. And for the year 1918 which just ended, the mine produced exactly 5,545 ounces, again, right on target, allowing for the doubled full-year throughput.

"But now let's look at the assay results. Every hole is different, which is to be expected, but nonetheless, not one of the new holes is less than two ounces per ton. We even have one running at over five ounces."

"So what do you do in a case like that? Work on the average?"

"Yes, that's probably fairest, and we'll throw out the highest and lowest holes just to be conservative. So the average works out to be two point five ounces per ton. At that grade, our output for 1918 here at the Revue should have been 17,000 ounces...."

"Leaving over eleven thousand ounces unaccounted for!"

"Samuel. I don't think I have to tell you what needs to be done. But remember, all that we've discussed this evening is just theory. We need to catch these buggers in the act of milling the contents of their lunch boxes. I leave that side of it to you. Just remember to involve Simcoe very closely or the magistrate will throw the case out. And if that bastard Frikkie Meyer is involved in any way, I want him nailed! I'll have his guts for fucking garters! Come on, let's go home, I'm sure Agnes would like to see her new husband for a change!"

Chapter 8

With the Revue riddle finally solved, or at least partially solved, and Blackie Schwartz not due back from Shamva for another four days, Samuel thought the time was now ripe to get to the bottom of the other matter that troubled him: The Warthog's Tusk murder.

Early the next morning Samuel phoned the police camp in Umtali asking for Barry Simcoe.

"Simcoe," said the young man's voice on the other end of the line.

"Ah, yes, Samuel Kumalo here. Did Mr. Thorneycroft fill you in on the autopsy findings for the Old Umtali mission body?"

"Yes he did and my hats off to you, Samuel, for pushing through with your gut feeling on that one. The boss just handed me your certificate of deputation from the magistrate's court. He said it wasn't easy and to get it through he had to agree to a time limitation. The magistrate's given you one year from yesterday."

"And is it limited to a particular case?"

"Let me see...hmm, no, no limitation there, only with respect to time."

Samuel was ecstatic. "Good," he said, "so that means I can be involved with you on the Revue gold theft scheme. Do you think we could meet out at Old Umtali Mission? Today? I want to take a look at the murder scene, or, should I rather say, where they found the body. And then I'll bring you up to date on Revue."

§

Old Umtali is one of those strange and serendipitous quirks of history that occur when lack of foresight and the powerful forces of capitalism collide. In the case of Old Umtali, as it afterwards came to be known, the first white settlers laid out a very pleasant, well-planned town, wide streets laid out in a grid, with several parks and lots reserved for churches, a library and even a city hall. Some twelve hundred families had already settled in the town when the townsfolk received terrible news from the railroad company building the railroad from the port of Beira on the Indian Ocean in Mozambique westward to Salisbury. There it would connect with the existing railroad to Bulawayo in Matabeleland and thence south down into the heartland of South Africa.

"Your new town's location is a problem for our engineers," the railway executives had said. "The grades are such that we will need at least two, maybe even three, locomotives to haul the train the ten miles from Machipanda on the Mozambique border, to Umtali. It just won't work. The only route that works for the railway is to bring it in behind

Christmas Pass. The closest station we can have to your town is almost ten miles away. So it's your choice. Stay where you are with no railroad station and haul all your goods from the railway by ox-wagon over Christmas Pass, or move your town to the other side of Christmas Pass and build a new town centred on the railway station."

There had been much murmuring and muttering, but in the end, and with some financial compensation from Cecil Rhodes' Chartered Company, the entire populace had moved their houses up over Christmas Pass to an extremely pretty location nestled between a semi-circular range of hills. And once the move was complete and the gardens re-planted, everyone agreed it had been a damned good idea to move!

The former town site began to be known as Old Umtali, but now, after almost thirty years, there was very little left to suggest there had ever been a town there. Ali Ibrahim and his son Ishmail still had a small general dealer's store, selling a wide variety of goods to the mainly African trade in the neighbourhood. And of course, there was the mission. The American Methodist Episcopal Church had been granted 'free and clear' ownership of 13,000 acres of land by Cecil Rhodes in 1892 to establish a mission station. Twenty-seven years later, the mission comprised a small hospital with an emergency room, a six bed maternity section and ten beds in five general care wards, as well as a church and a primary school. It was to this latter group of buildings that Samuel headed on his Royal Enfield after arriving at the mission gates and being pointed in the right direction by the gateman. He had told Samuel to ask for Mr. Sykes, the school principal.

As Samuel walked past the open windows of the class rooms he could see that the classrooms were empty, the children probably away on holiday. He made for the administrative block and there on a plain wooden door was a painted sign that read 'R.W.Sykes M.A (Hons)'. Samuel rapped lightly, and a deep voice called out, "Come".

Ronald Sykes was a short, plumpish man, probably mid-fifties, Samuel judged, with pince-nez glasses perched on a sharp, longish nose. He was balding and trying to hide it by brushing long strands of grey hair across his pate. From Samuel's considerable height advantage, Sykes' attempts at follicular camouflage were totally wasted, and merely looked like a giant ghost spider attacking his pinkish scalp.

After Samuel had introduced himself, Sykes pointed to a wooden chair and, with a broad Southern American accent, asked him to please sit.

They talked a little about the weather and about the recently ended war. (Sykes told of how he had a son who had arrived in France on a troopship just three days after the armistice was signed). Samuel shared a few of his experiences in both France and East Africa, much to Sykes' surprise. He had not realised how wide-ranging the war had been in East Africa. He had only recently arrived from Nashville, Tennessee. Samuel found it a little difficult to follow the man's broad southern accent.

Finally, Samuel brought the conversation around to the death of Gideon Munyaradzi, showing Sykes his certificate of deputisation. It was clear from the conversation that Sykes was under the impression that Gideon's death was purely accidental. Samuel planned on keeping it that way, at least for the time being.

"Mr. Sykes, I have been asked by the Umtali police to initiate a file for the deceased, and I was hoping you could help me."

"Sure. Can do. But remember that I've only been here for a little over a year, but I'll surely tell y'all whatever I can."

"Thank-you, sir, you are very kind. First, I understand that Gideon worked here. Do you have his personal details, date of birth, address etcetera?"

Sykes got up from his swivel chair and opened a green metal final cabinet, extracting a blue file. He sat back down behind his desk and started riffling through the papers in the file.

"Says here he was born on January 14th, 1895. He would have been twenty-four this week. Too bad. His address is given as care of a Mrs. Hilda Munyaradzi at the Rezende Mine, but I know that he actually lived in staff quarters here at the Mission."

"His mother lives at the Rezende Mine. She is the widow of a man who died a few years ago in an underground accident. The mine owner allows her to continue living in the staff quarters."

"Hmmm. Seems accidents follow this family around."

"What was his job here, Mr. Sykes?"

"Why, bless my soul, I thought you knew. He was a teacher, and a darned good one I should add. He had recently applied for the vacant position of Deputy Headmaster. The timing of this whole business is just so, so sad. Only yesterday I received a message from our church headquarters in Dallas advising me that his application had been successful. I guess we'll have to begin the search again. School starts up in three weeks; I hope we have enough time."

"Who were the other applicants?" asked Samuel, trying to keep his interest low-key, but in his heart he felt a flicker of hope that herein might lay the seeds of a motive. Because right now he had nothing but a dead body, some unusual wounds and a nasty poison. Suspects: NIL. Means: poison. How administered: unknown. Motive: NIL

Sykes retrieved a second file from the cabinet.

"There were two other applicants. Isobel Takwanda was one, the other was Zebediah Tongarara."

"What happened to the previous Deputy?"

"Oh, nothing really. He was promoted to be headmaster of one of our mission schools down Fort Victoria way. You can see him if you wish to, he only leaves tomorrow."

Samuel made a note, but waved his hand dismissively.

"Do you know if Gideon had any enemies? Who were his friends, acquaintances? I'm trying to develop a picture of this man, a man I never met."

"Enemies? No I don't think so. He was a very well-liked young man, never spoke ill of anyone, but he was very clever, you know, and had completed a number of ancillary courses. On the negative side, I got the impression that he didn't suffer fools lightly, if you know what I mean. And he was very, very conservative in his views. More conservative than I think I was at his age."

"And as for friends and acquaintances," the Principal continued, "I don't really know. I know he used to socialise a little with the ladies on the staff. I got the impression that he was looking for a wife. You should mebbe rather talk to some of the other teachers. They would know better than I about girlfriends and so on."

"And you, Mr. Sykes? Where were you when Gideon lost his life? Say between seven o'clock and eight o'clock last Tuesday evening?"

"Why, where I am every evening at that time. In the chapel. Praying. And now if you don't mind, I have a lot of preparation to do for the new school year"

"You've been very helpful, Mr. Sykes. One more question perhaps?"

Sykes nodded his head, his glasses slipping a little on the beads of sweat which were accumulating in the creases of his nose. Samuel put it down to being a fairly warm day.

"Can you or one of your staff direct me to where Gideon's body was found?"

"It was the night-watchman who found him." Sykes glanced at his watch. "It's still another hour before he comes on duty. I'll send someone down to his cottage to fetch him. He should be awake by now."

"Thank you very much, Mr. Sykes." And Samuel shook the head-master's hand, noting how damp it was. Damp and cold to the touch. Samuel was reminded of a barbel, never knowing how much Mr. Sykes loved eating catfish straight out of the Cumberland River. Catfish and barbel – one and the same; different countries, different names, that's all.

§

As Samuel left Mr. Sykes's office he heard the sound of a motor-cycle approaching. The tone of its engine was different to the Royal Enfield engine he had become used to. It was an Indian, and on it, arriving in a cloud of dust, wearing war-surplus aviator goggles, was Barry Simcoe.

"Glad you could come," said Samuel. "I've just finished interviewing the headmaster and now I'm ready to head over to meet the man who found the body. Did you remember to bring a camera?"

§

Despite the heat of the afternoon, the night-watchman was wearing a thick black coat like a cloak of office. Pinned to its left lapel with a silver safety pin was a medal made of some light metal, possibly aluminum. Without wanting to seem too curious, Samuel could make out a cross on the medal and surmised that it denoted the old man's membership of some religious organisation.

The night-watchman, who told them his name was Lucas, was fairly tall, and had a dignified stance, with a lined face, his hair quite white. Walking slowly, almost painfully, he led Samuel and Simcoe over to a copse of trees growing in and around a jumble of rocks, the kind of outcrop that in southern Africa has come to be known as a *kopje*. One of the rocks was a granite giant, pockmarked by weather, with yellow and grey lichen staining it, and alongside the rock, almost caressing it with clasping branches, grew a grey-barked ironwood tree. Its wood was true to its name, and no woodsman would ever try to fell one of these trees without at least three axes, a sharpening stone and a good deal of sweat to spare. Way down at the bottom of the huge rock, protected from the elements by a small natural overhanging ledge, were a number of bushmen paintings. Beautiful, red and ochre-coloured, two-dimensional renditions of sable antelope, kudu and giraffe and here and there, skinny stick figures of humans, some with spears and others with bows.

"Here it was," said Lucas slowly, pointing with a finger badly disfigured with arthritis. "His feet were here, and his head over here," and the old man slowly made his indications. Samuel had taken out his spiral-bound notebook and was busy sketching the area. Barry had set up a tripod and was taking photographs of the scene.

Samuel bent down low to the ground and could see dark stains in the sparsely-grassed, sandy soil and assumed them to be bloodstains. He walked carefully around the area, eyes peeled for anything out of the ordinary.

And then he saw it. A small square piece of cloth, white in colour, its edge neatly hemmed and stitched to prevent the cloth from fraying. Samuel thought that the stitching looked as though it had been done by hand. The hankie, for that is what he took it to be, was lying close to the huge ironwood tree atop brown leaves, small sheets of bark and drying grass. He called to Barry to photograph it in situ, then stooped to retrieve it, and as he did so a zephyr of wind fanned the dried leaves. He felt a shiver down his spine. This place has the feel of a spirit being present, he thought. A homeless spirit. Perhaps one of those hunters from the rock painting over there. He shivered again.

Samuel handed the cloth to Simcoe with a mumbled 'bag it', then turned back to Lucas.

"Lucas, it was you who told the undertakers that he had been gored by a warthog. How did you know it was a warthog and not some other animal?" he asked the old man.

"Because I found the tusk."

"What? Where? Here by the body?"

"No. It was a little way back over there, towards the school." The old man waved over in the direction from whence they had come. "It was hidden under a small bush."

"How did you know it was the tusk that had done the injury?"

"Because it still had fresh blood on it. That's how I found it. The buzzing of the flies."

"And where is this tusk now?"

"At my house. Do you want it?"

"Yes, of *course* I do. It might be very important evidence."

Making allowance for the old man's arthritic feet, they walked slowly to a collection of small thatched cottages. Before they arrived Lucas called out what sounded like a stream of instructions and a young girl came running holding a blue cloth in her hand.

"This is my grand-daughter," said Lucas. "Charity, this is Mister Kumalo, from the Rezende Mine in Penhalonga. Oh, and also Mr. Simcoe, a *mapolisa* from Umtali."

Charity curtseyed in the very traditional and polite Shona manner that young ladies reserve for their elders. She looked to be about fifteen, pretty and with a very nice, well-developed figure. At her grandfather's direction, she handed the blue cloth to Samuel, who opened it carefully and saw a yellowing, razor-sharp, slightly curved tusk with a dark brown substance painting its surface from the tip backwards for at least three or four inches. Samuel knew that Doc Snelgar would relish determining if this was the very tusk that had caused the jagged wounds in Gideon's backside and groin.

"So, Charity. Do you go to school here?" asked Samuel.

"I did before, but not now. Now I am a senior," she said proudly, "I go now to school in Umtali. I am going into form two at the Sakubva High School."

"Where do you live when you are attending school?"

"With my *babamukuru*. My father's elder brother. He works at the post office in Umtali. He delivers mail."

"Hau," said Samuel, "that is a very important job. Did you know Gideon, Charity? The man whose body your grandfather found?"

Charity looked down at the ground. Was it fear or grief? "Yes, he was my teacher until one year ago, here at the mission elementary school." She had begun to cry, her eyes spilling large teardrops.

"Was he a good teacher, Charity? Kind?"

"He was very, very good. So helpful to all of us with his time for extra lessons and so on. And yes, he was a very kind man." Now the girl was openly weeping, large teardrops falling from her eyes darkening spots on the dry earth at her feet.

"Do you think he had any enemies? Anyone who would wish him harm?"

"Never! Everyone liked him, respected him. But there is one fellow-teacher of his who seemed to have fallen out with him." She fisted her eyes, clearing the tears.

"And who was that?"

"Isobel Takwanda. I have seen them having words, very strong words."

Samuel thanked the couple for their time and bid them farewell as he and Simcoe began the long walk back to the mission school where they had left their motorcycles. Samuel had a lot to think about, and before he had a single pint of Agnes' beer tonight, every last word he had heard today must be written down in his spiral note-book.

"Mister Barry, I'm going to be heading off home to Penhalonga now. I know that protocol says you should take the tusk with you and enter it into the evidence log, but I want to examine it a little more closely. I'll bring it to Doc Snelgar tomorrow, if that's OK?"

As he kicked the reluctant Royal Enfield to life beneath him, and Simcoe roared off back to Umtali on his Indian, Samuel suddenly realised that he had forgotten to ask old Lucas one very important question. He levered the bike into gear and headed along a back road towards the old man's house.

Lucas was sitting on a wooden stool outside his small thatched cottage eating a bowl of *sadza,* the stiff maize-meal porridge so loved by the Shona people.

"*Baba,*" said Samuel politely. The old man looked up from his bowl, his eyes tired and red. "Excuse me for interrupting your meal. I forgot to ask you a very important question. I am not from around here, I come from Bulawayo. That's why I don't know the answer myself.

The question I have is, have you ever seen a warthog around here? On this mission property? Anywhere close?"

And the old man just shook his head, and swallowed what he had in his mouth.

"Those animals. They much prefer hotter climates don't they? Like down towards the Sabi and the Lundi and the Nuanetsi Rivers. Not around here?"

The old man merely nodded.

Samuel headed home. Agnes would be wondering what had happened to him.

Chapter 9

After his supper, and having surprised Agnes by refusing her offer of a large mug of thick, foaming gruel beer, Samuel continued sitting at their small dining-room table. Together with four straight-backed chairs, it had been given to them as a wedding present by Eddie and Bella. He took out his Croxley spiral-bound ruled notebook and a fountain pen and on the front of it in his best copper-plate, mission-school-taught script, wrote the words:

Case No. 1. Gideon Munyaradzi. The Warthog's Tusk

Then he flipped open the book and began writing his notes on the page following his sketch of the murder scene. He had filled four pages before he was done, his eyes sore and tired. The tusk sat on the table in front of him, still in its blue tea-cloth wrapping. Tomorrow, decided Samuel. I'll look at it tomorrow under the morning sun.

§

Samuel slept fitfully that night, his mind full of horrible images: a dead body lying on its stomach, pants torn open and blood showing in the wounds. The face of a warthog, perhaps the ugliest of all God's creatures, a warthog with two viciously curved large upper tusks, and two shorter and straighter, razor-sharp lower tusks, one of which was missing. He tossed and turned. What have I missed? he kept asking himself.

And then, suddenly, the sun was shining through the bedroom window, weaver birds were arguing in their colony of nests in the tall *Msasa* tree outside. He could hear Hastings in the kitchen with Agnes, carrying on a high-pitched, almost one-sided conversation in which every second sentence started with *why*? Samuel smiled. My boy is sure to become a good policeman, he thought. He never stops asking questions!

While Agnes prepared breakfast, thick squares of brown bread soaked in milk with a sprinkling of white sugar on top, Samuel went out onto the small verandah that sheltered the front door of their mine cottage, holding his son in the crook of an arm. He held the cloth-covered tusk in his other hand. Once outside, he uncovered the tusk and allowed the bright early-morning sun to play upon it. Hastings' little fingers reached out for the tusk, but Samuel kept it away from him.

The tusk was not large; no more than twelve inches in length, but one side was as sharp as any steel knife sharpened for hours upon a fine-grained whet-stone. He could clearly see the dried blood on the pointed end of the tusk and wondered if Gideon had felt any pain. Just then his father-in-law arrived, clumping up in his rubber boots and blue overalls, ready for another day underground.

"What have you got there, Samuel?"

"Evidence, *Baba,*" replied Samuel. "That Gideon Munyaradzi case, you know."

"Oh yes. Is that from the warthog that gored him?"

"I think so, but how will we ever know for sure? It was found some distance from the body, but, as you can see, it does have what appears to be blood on it."

Amos came in close and peered over Samuel's shoulder.

"It's not the main tusk," he opined, squinting short-sightedly through presbyopian eyes. "It's one of the lower teeth; they are smaller than the upper ones, less curved. And very sharp, too." He used his index finger to point at the sharpened edge of the tusk. "It get's sharpened against the larger upper tusk. Every time the warthog chews or bites something, the two tusks grind against each other, leaving the small one, this one, razor-sharp."

Samuel was beginning to view his father-in-law in a new light. For a simple Shona tribesman, he certainly knew a lot about wild-life. And badly needed to see an optometrist about his eyes.

"And have you ever seen a warthog in these parts?"

"No, not around here. Further south, where the Odzi meets the Sabi in Chief Maranke's area, yes, there I have seen them. And you know, Samuel, warthogs are not very aggressive animals. They always run when they see a human. Unless it is a female protecting her young, of course. I always thought that story of Gideon being killed

94

by a warthog a little farfetched and difficult to believe. But now I must go, my crew is waiting for me. I just wanted to say good morning to Agnes and Shadreck."

After his father-in-law had left Samuel called Agnes out onto the verandah.

"Agnes. I am very disappointed. Why did you not tell your father that my son's name is now Hastings? Not Shadreck."

Agnes looked forlorn. "I am sorry, my husband, truly sorry. But you see, my father considered it such a great honour that his first grandson should be named after his late brother. I didn't want to break his heart over such a small thing as a name."

Samuel said no more. He knew she was right, but he also knew that he owed so much to Hastings Follett, that in a way he considered him more a brother than any of the male children of his own mother.

§

A half-hour later, newly washed and shaved, and dressed in brown woolen slacks and a tweed jacket with leather patches on the elbows that he had been given to him by a British officer in France, Samuel fired up the Royal Enfield and headed off for Umtali and a meeting with Doc. Snelgar. He knew he had a few days to devote to the Gideon case before he would need to turn his attention back to Revue. Blackie Schwartz's enforced absence would come to an end on Friday or Saturday.

Doc Snelgar looked up from his Remington typewriter as Samuel swung the Medical Examiner's room door open on its springs.

"Samuel? Trooper Simcoe said I should be expecting you." Snelgar stood up. "Fancy a mug of tea?"

They walked back along the corridor to the nurses' wardroom, a venue renowned for its tea and coffee. The place was empty so Samuel put the kettle on to boil while Doc Snelgar rummaged around for tea leaves to put into the six-cup china tea-pot.

A few minutes later, sipping their teas, Samuel came straight to the point. "I have found what I believe may be the murder weapon, Doctor."

"Murder weapon? In the Munyaradzi case, you mean? How can you even be sure what the murder weapon is?"

"Well, the deceased was gored by something, supposedly a warthog, and I have been provided with a warthog's tusk found not far from the body. What is more, there's blood on the tusk."

"Let me take a look at the evil instrument." Snelgar held out his hand, and Samuel handed him the blue cloth parcel.

"Hmm," said Snelgar, turning the tusk this way and that in exactly the same manner that Samuel had done not many hours earlier.

"Yes, indeed, this could very well be the instrument that caused the deceased's wounds, but we need to do this scientifically. Come." With that Snelgar got up, and with the tusk in one hand and a mug half full of tea in the other, he strode down the green-painted corridor towards his autopsy rooms.

Gideon's newly-exhumed body was in a refrigeration drawer. As Snelgar opened the drawer Samuel couldn't help thinking how peaceful the dead man looked.

"You know, Samuel, when I was in South Africa during the Boer War I worked alongside a very interesting medical man. Conan-Doyle was his name. He has written a number of stories about a detective named Sherlock Holmes. I have found his methods of investigation to be very intriguing. You may want to borrow a book or two and read them. You could learn a lot from them, even though they are fictional tales. If you're at all interested I'll bring them in from my digs."

Samuel smiled. "Thank you, Doctor, but I have already read everything Conan-Doyle has written. In France I was billeted for a while in a large house that had a very extensive library, including many books by Conan-Doyle. I have a copy of A Study in Scarlet at my house."

Snelgar shook his head in seeming amazement. One learns something new every day, he thought. Then he turned his attention back to the tusk.

A few minutes later Snelgar nodded his head and said, "I am quite sure that the wounds in his groin and buttocks were caused by this tusk. The fit is incredibly precise. I also want to type-test the blood against the deceased's blood, make sure it's his. However, I am pretty sure, as we discussed, that these wounds were *not* the cause of death, and I can find no evidence that the tusk was used to deliver a dose of potassium cyanide. Frankly, I suspect these wounds were inflicted simply to throw a potential investigator off the track. And whoever did this was almost successful. If you hadn't stuck your nose into this, Samuel, young Gideon would have moldered forever in his grave without anyone knowing how he really met his end, or indeed that he was even murdered."

"Yes, Doc, but I am still no further towards a solution than when you told me he had been poisoned. I have no suspects, not even a person of interest. Nothing, zero." And Samuel thumped the table with his fist in frustration.

"What about the last person to have seen him? Or the person who found his body?"

"I have no idea who was the last to see him, and the person who found his body is an old night-watchman with misshapen fingers, who can barely walk. I doubt he would be physically able to hold that tusk, let alone knock a twenty-five year old man down with a blow to the head."

"Well, then, Samuel old son, you've got your work cut out for you."

§

The next item on Samuel's agenda was to have a quick chat with Barry Simcoe, back at the Police camp. He was in his small office down the corridor from Superintendent Thorneycroft, whose door was closed.

"I wanted to bring you up to date on my two cases," said Samuel. "There have been big developments on one and virtually nothing on the other."

After finishing his synopsis of the Revue case, he said, "The mine manager gets back to the mine this weekend. I can't be sure, but Mr. Evans and I suspect that he will want to start milling the stolen ore soon after his arrival. If we can catch him and his cronies in the act you will need to be close by to make the formal arrests."

"What do you want me to do?" asked Simcoe.

"Can you come out to Rezende on Saturday afternoon? Mr. and Mrs. Evans will give you a bed for the night. I think they will start milling the ore on Sunday evening after the graveyard shift has gone underground. They only have a few tons of ore to grind, maybe eight or ten hours worth."

"How will they extract the gold?" asked Simcoe.

"As the ore is milled the slurry will be run over copper sheets coated with mercury. The mercury dissolves the gold in the slurry."

"Then how do they get the gold out of the mercury?"

"They'll either use a piece of chamois leather or, more likely, the retort that's in the laboratory. They heat up the amalgam to such a temperature that the mercury vaporises into a gas leaving the gold behind in the retort."

"Isn't mercury gas dangerous?" asked Simcoe.

"Oh yes, very, very dangerous, but they don't let it escape into the atmosphere. They use a retort to condense the gas back into liquid mercury and it is then re-used again and again."

"And what about the chamois-leather? How does that work?"

"They place the mercury-gold amalgam in a square of this special leather that comes from a wild goat that is found in the French Pyrenees. It is then folded up and squeezed very tightly. For some strange reason the mercury passes through the leather but the gold remains behind."

"How do you know all this, Samuel? Were you a gold-miner before you became a policeman?"

"No," Samuel replied with a hearty laugh. "I have been studying at the feet of the gold guru of Penhalonga – my boss, Eddie Evans." They both laughed at the thought of a six foot three inch Samuel as Kipling's Kim, sitting *chela–* like at the feet of a five foot six inch Tibetan lama in the form of Eddie Evans.

"And, unfortunately, as you know Barry, we don't have much to report on the Munyaradzi case. I have received confirmation from Doc Snelgar that this tusk," and he handed over the piece of ivory still wrapped in the original blue cloth, "is most probably the weapon used in the Munyaradzi attack. You need to log this in as evidence. Doc Snelgar will be providing a formal report saying that based on tests he ran on the body, this tusk in all likelihood created the various wounds in the front and back of the body. All he needs to do now is a blood typing to confirm everything."

Simcoe took the cloth parcel gingerly, holding it as though its contents were made of some fine ceramic.

"So what's your plan going forward?"

"When I leave here I'll call in at the mission again on my way back to Rezende. There are a couple of Gideon's friends I want to interview. I didn't have time to see them yesterday. I wonder if you could help me in the investigation?"

"Of course. The boss," and Simcoe nodded his head towards Thorneycroft's office, "told me to give you every assistance. So no need to ask, I'm here to help."

"Thank you, you're very kind. I need to find out where one can obtain potassium cyanide. It might be easier for you as a policeman than for me as a private individual."

Simcoe was writing rapidly on a small pad.

"Sure thing, Samuel. Any idea where I could start?"

"Eddie Evans told me that certain mines use cyanide in their gold extraction process, so it might have come from that source. Having said that, however, Eddie doesn't know of any mines in our particular district that use cyanide. Anyway, maybe you could start with a mining supply company. Like Daggit & Sons on Main Street, for example."

"Fine, thanks, I'll start there."

"And since you'll be in the vicinity, drop in to Mitchell's Pharmacy. They're on the same street. Old Jock Mitchell might have an idea. But don't tell either of the businesses why you need the information. Just say something like 'to assist in our enquiries'. I want to keep the actual cause of death under wraps for the time being. It's a significant part of the case."

"Got it, mum's the word." And Simcoe ran his finger over his lips in a sealing motion.

§

Samuel was getting the feel of the Royal Enfield. Its broader tires made it more stable yet, paradoxically, less easy to handle in sand than the narrower-wheeled Indian on which he had learned to ride with Hastings Follett four years earlier. Even though he had ridden army-issue Royal Enfield bikes during his eighteen month sojourn in France, it had always seemed to be in conditions of thick, viscous, mud or on metalled French and Belgian roads, never the fine sand of Rhodesian trails. There had now been a few days of bright sunshine without any rain, quite unusual for Umtali in late January, the height of the rainy season. As a result, the main Umtali – Salisbury road leading over Christmas Pass was as dry as tinder and Samuel kept the throttle open all the way to the top of the pass, a cloud of dust billowing out behind him. When gravity took over on the downward stretch, he slackened off the throttle, but, with grade and momentum kicking in, the bike kept increasing speed. As he reached the bottom of the pass and the road flattened out, Samuel glanced down and noticed the needle was at its furthest point on the speedometer, well over sixty miles per hour. The wind was whistling in his ears and flapping the lapels of his tweed jacket.

He was travelling so fast that he almost missed the turnoff to Penhalonga and as a result was forced to brake sharply and turn at the same time, never a good thing to do on a motor-cycle. Compounding the problem was a twelve inch high ridge of sand created by the wheels of other vehicles that had made the same right-hand turn. Suddenly the Royal Enfield's back wheel flipped out from underneath him, and Samuel parted company with the machine, the bike wobbling drunkenly into the long grass by the side of the road. Samuel slid on his belly right over the road, landing spread-eagled halfway into a shallow drainage ditch. For a moment he couldn't move or even breathe, the wind having been knocked out of him. Then, when he tried to turn over, he felt an excruciating, stabbing pain in his lower back, and blacked out where he lay, with birds singing in the mimosa tree growing alongside the road and the hot midday sun beating down on the back of his head and neck.

He had lain there for about ten minutes when a passing motorist found him. It was Mrs. Pennefather in her green Crossley tourer. She had purchased the car after her husband died and had employed a chauffeur to drive it for her. That day she had an appointment to meet with her bank manager in Umtali. She was admiring the view from the expansive back seat of the car, the canvas roof pulled up to shade her from the fierce rays of an African sun shining from cloudless blue skies.

"Sunday!" she shouted, tapping urgently on the driver's shoulder. "There's a body lying by the side of the road back there. Stop!"

Sunday came to a stop amid a billowing cloud of dust, and then backed the car up thirty yards to where Samuel was lying. Mrs. Pennefather leapt out of the Crossley with an agility that belied her eighty-two years of age. She knelt down next to Samuel and tentatively touched his shoulder. She recognized him immediately. "Samuel," she called out. "Samuel, are you alright?"

At this, Samuel began to come to, flexing his arms and legs to make sure there was nothing broken. The pain in his back had subsided somewhat, but he was still unsure whether or not he should roll over. Sunday had by now joined the old lady, and with much grunting, managed to lift Samuel slowly and unsteadily to a standing position.

"Here, Samuel, come and get in my car. I'm going to take you to the mission hospital; it's only a short distance from here. Let the doctor there take a look at you. Just to make sure you're absolutely alright."

The mission hospital was a bright and airy building, with white-washed walls and shiny waxed cement floors. Two porters held Samuel under his armpits and manoeuvred him carefully onto a high hospital bed in a room marked EXAMINATON.

Two minutes after lying down on the hard bed, and having bid farewell to Mrs. Pennefather and Sunday, thanking them again for their kindness in stopping, in walked a young black man in a white laboratory jacket, a stethoscope slung loosely around his neck and a strange looking instrument strapped to his forehead. Samuel very quickly discovered its purpose. It was a lamp with a very intense and focused beam of light. The doctor was an elegant-looking young man, not much past thirty in Samuel's estimation. He introduced himself as 'Dr. Eli Jefferson, Dallas, Texas'. He had short, straight black hair, richly pomaded with Brilliantine. He performed several tests on Samuel. They included the liberal use of a small rubber-tipped hammer on his knees and he ran the lamp's bright beam back and forth over his eyes, before eventually pronouncing himself satisfied with his patient's health.

"I was concerned that you might have a concussion," he said, "but all my tests have come back negative. Your back, though, is another story. I can see from the graze marks on your abdomen that you impacted the ground with your hip and slid a few yards on your side before ending up sliding on your stomach. I suspect you may have suffered a hairline fracture of your pelvis which accounts for the lower back pain you're experiencing when you try to move. Normally, I'd do a series of X-rays, but our mobile machine is out of action right now, the X-Ray tube has burnt out. We *do* have a spare tube, but we don't have the expertise to install it here at the mission. It had to be sent in to Umtali to be installed. I've been told it'll be back tomorrow, so I'd like you to stay overnight until we can get the X-rays done. However, on the bright side, you have

105

none of the other symptoms normally associated with a pelvic fracture. No shooting pains in your legs, no blood in your urine, so I'm hoping that you've just hurt the ligaments that hold your pelvis together. We'll know much more tomorrow morning. I suggest that you relax, take the painkillers I've prescribed and try to sleep."

"Thank you very much, doctor. Do you think someone could phone through to the Rezende Mine and tell Mr. Evans where I am, and what happened? He will get a message through to my wife. Oh, and doctor, I think my motor-cycle is in the long grass not far from where I was picked up. I am worried it may be stolen."

"Leave it with me," said the Texan then abruptly turned and marched off, no doubt to attend to his other patients. Samuel had seen quite a number of women with small children in a waiting room as he was helped into the examination room.

Samuel dozed off, dreaming of the wind whistling in his ears as he flew down Christmas Pass. With the benefit of hindsight he knew exactly what he had done wrong and felt utterly foolish at having made the stupid mistake of braking sharply on a tight curve in deep sand.

He was awoken from his reverie by a stern-looking, large-breasted, middle-aged black woman, reading glasses perched halfway down her nose. The highly-polished brass badge on her stiff-starched nurse's uniform proclaimed her to be Sister Lydia Mukarakate RN. Samuel recognised the surname. He had come across it on one of his investigations before the war, while with the BSAP. He suspected that she was from the Mrewa district in Mashonaland, a true *Muzezuru* rather than a *Samanyika* from Manicaland.

She handed him a paper envelope with two pills inside and a glass of water with which to swallow them.

"I have phoned to your Mr. Evans and told him what happened to you. He was very concerned. He wanted to organise an ambulance to take you to Umtali General, but I told him that your care here would be far better than the government hospital."

"Sister, please forgive my forwardness, but are you a member of the Mangwende family, from Mrewa?"

Sister Lydia was quite taken aback at this question.

"Yes," she replied, nodding her head, "I am married to Chief Mangwende's younger brother. But you, Mr. Kumalo, your name is well known as that of the Matabele royal family, from Matabeleland. How does a Matabele know about the Mangwendes?"

"I confess that I know the name from my previous work as a constable in the BSAP. A certain Jameson Mukarakate was the main subject of one of my dockets." He had wanted to say 'suspect' rather than subject, but he sensed that in his present position, diplomacy might be his greatest asset.

Lydia laughed out loud, her rather ample bosom jiggling with her mirth. She used her index finger to push her glasses back up her nose.

"Ah yes, that Jameson! We like to think of him as the black sheep of the family, although in Shona we do not say sheep, we prefer the word goat - *mbudzi*. There were no sheep in Rhodesia until the white man came. No, we call him the orphaned goat. But he is a likeable rogue."

"You are right, mother, and likeable for sure, but nevertheless with a great liking for bending the laws, especially those pertaining to stray cattle."

"I have not seen Jameson for some time now, but I believe that he is still a free man, no charges pending against him."

"I couldn't say, *amai*, I have been away at the war for four years, and now that I am back I am no longer with the BSAP. I work for Mr. Eddie Evans at the Rezende Mine."

There was a pause while the older woman fluffed up Samuel's pillows. She seemed like a good sort, not given to undue gossip, and best of all, thought Samuel, she is not a local. Her town is at least one hundred miles from here. Maybe she can help me.

"*Amai*," he began, very courteously, using the Shona word for mother, "did you hear of the death of that poor young teacher from the mission school?"

"Au, yes, what a shame! He was such a nice boy, and very clever, too. They say he would have become the deputy head of the school under Mr. Sykes. And at such a young age, too."

"I heard that he died from a warthog attack?"

108

"Yes, that's what they are saying, but myself, I cannot believe it. A warthog would rather run away squealing than stand and fight. They are not so very aggressive. And when last can anyone remember a warthog living in this area? No, I think that Gideon's death should have been more closely investigated before his body was so quickly buried. I don't want to seem like a busybody, but that girl Isobel should have been investigated. I don't trust that one." And the sister waggled her finger from side to side.

"Isobel Takwanda? Gideon's fellow teacher at the mission school?"

"Yes, that very one. You could see that Gideon loved her, and she appeared to return his love, but only on *her* terms. With her it was me, me, me." The nurse tapped her foot on the cement floor for emphasis. "A very self-centred young lady. And very easy-going with her affections."

"What do you mean?"

"Well, I have seen her visiting here at the hospital. I suspect that she and Dr. Jefferson are more than just friends."

Samuel was starting to get the feeling that the pain and discomfort of his accident was starting to pay dividends in the form of information.

Samuel remembered the third applicant for the Deputy Headmaster job. "And what about Zebediah Tongarara?" he asked. "Did he get along with Gideon?"

"That Zebediah! Au! He is nothing. No brains, no drive, nothing compared to Gideon. And now that Gideon is gone, I am sure that Zebediah will get the Deputy position."

"What about Isobel? Wasn't she also in the running for that job?"

"Oh yes, I heard that story. But remember, Mister Kumalo, she is a woman. These American Methodists who run this mission are very, very conservative. I just don't think a woman would have been given the job."

From zero suspects this morning, Samuel now had a notebook full.

And motives galore. As the great detective Sir Basil Thomson of Scotland Yard once said, "The search for the motive should be kept up incessantly, for no murder was ever committed without a motive. There is *always* an underlying motive."

Chapter 10

Samuel had no idea what Sister Lydia's little white pills contained, but they certainly seemed to have done an excellent job. His back still hurt but not nearly as badly as it had done an hour or so before, and he felt that he should really be getting back to Agnes. But the good American doctor would not hear of it. He insisted that Samuel stay through the night so that his health could be monitored for a full twenty-four period as stipulated in the best medical journals. And, of course, there were still the X-Rays to be taken.

Finally, the two of them reached a compromise: Samuel would stay on condition that he could interview Gideon's two colleagues, Isobel Takwanda and Zebediah Tongarara. It was now just after three o'clock in the afternoon and Jefferson promised that he would arrange for the first of the two interviewees to be at the hospital at four o'clock. The school complex was a mere half mile from the hospital.

In the interim, Sister Lydia had reported to her patient that his motor-cycle had been found in the long grass close to where the accident had occurred, and that a young herd-boy had wheeled it up to the hospital. The young man's status amongst his fellow herd-boys had risen enormously as a result of the great responsibility he had been entrusted with. The young lad was now standing outside the front door of the hospital, meagrely clad in cast-off clothes, holding the bike upright. Samuel peered out the window and slowly and clearly explained to the lad how the kick-stand worked. Finally the young boy managed to get the heavy metal stand to click down to the ground and to balance the big olive-green machine on it. It was quite remarkable that he succeeded, for the motor-cycle was considerably heavier than he.

"*Mukomana* – young lad," called Samuel loudly, "come here. I have something for you." He fished in his trousers where they were draped over a chair and retrieved a silver coin. When the young boy was outside his window, Samuel flipped the coin to him. That silver half-crown was probably more money than the youngster had ever seen in his life.

"One more thing before you go, *mukomana*, how would you like to make four more of those coins?" and the two began to whisper softly through the hospital window.

§

"Good afternoon, *sisi, maswerasei?* You are Isobel?"

"Yes, sir, my name is Isobel Takwanda." Samuel could see she was nervous and he hadn't even really begun questioning her yet. She was a pleasant-looking young lady, her hair painstakingly done up in corn-rows tightly

112

laced with black thread. She wore horn-rimmed spectacles that added a certain air of intellectuality to an otherwise ordinary looking face. She was of medium height with a build that hinted at a future heaviness. She was fidgeting, alternately standing with her weight on either leg. Samuel decided not to offer her a seat. Let her sweat a bit, he thought.

"*Kumushakwako ndekupi?* Where is your *musha*, your home village, and date of birth, please?"

"I am from Melsetter District, my father is Dominic Takwanda. Like me, he is a teacher. My birth-date is April 17, 1896. In three months I shall be twenty-three."

"Good, good. Please Isobel, just try to relax. I am trying to get to the bottom of this affair of Gideon's death, and to do that I need to talk to everyone who knew him or had dealings with him. And since you worked with him I thought, 'who could there be better to tell me about Gideon than his friend, Isobel.' You *were* his friend, weren't you, Isobel?"

"Oh yes, of course. Yes we were friends. I would say we were perhaps *more* than friends. We were betrothed. We had made certain promises of marriage. Not immediate, you understand, but in the future."

"Were you lovers?"

"No, it had not come to that. Not yet. No, but we have been very close on a few occasions, close, but no sex."

Samuel understood. What a western teenager would term 'heavy petting' was fairly common in Shona culture. However, like many other cultures, sexual intercourse before marriage was very much frowned upon, especially in a mission station setting.

"Gideon had applied for the Deputy Head position. Did this bother you, since you had also applied and only one person could be successful?"

"Oh no. I knew I had no chance of getting the job. Mr. Sykes instructed me to apply. To make the applicant list bigger, he said, so that the church board in America wouldn't think that there was only one applicant."

"Do you know if Gideon had any enemies, anyone who might wish him dead?"

"But Gideon died from a warthog attack. Why would you ask if he had any enemies? But no, he did not, at least none that I knew of. He was a very nice man, well-liked by everyone." And Isobel began to cry, fishing out a small white linen hankie from under her dress sleeve to dab at her tears.

"Was he jealous at all? Jealous of your relationships with other men?"

"What do you mean? What other men? I have no other men. I am a good girl!" Isobel seemed genuinely indignant at this line of questioning.

"So your visits with Doctor Jefferson here at the hospital were purely professional?"

The look on Isobel's face betrayed her. Her eyes, formerly so steady in their gaze as she spoke with Samuel, now became shifty. Tiny beads of sweat had broken out on her forehead. The look in her eyes said: 'what does this man know?'

"Er, yes, professional, yes, related to a medical condition I have. Or, should I say, had, past tense."

"And what was that?"

"It was of a feminine nature." And she began twisting her hankie feverishly around her index finger.

She is lying, thought Samuel. *Lying through her teeth* as Eddie Evans would say.

§

"Yes, that is me, Zebediah Tongarara. My birth-date is July 4th, 1895. Doctor Jefferson said I will always have good luck because I was born on American day."

"American day? What on earth do you think he meant by that?"

"He said it is the day that America celebrates her victory over King Georgie."

Samuel, who had met a few Americans in France, mainly ambulance drivers, now realised that Zebediah was talking about Independence Day. This man is certainly not one of the brightest stars in the firmament, he thought.

"So, Zebediah. You knew Gideon personally, yes?"

"Oh yes, for sure. We have been teachers here for three years together. But he was here one year before me. He was my senior."

"Was he your friend?"

"Yes, he was. I cannot say a close friend; more like a good acquaintance."

"And soon to be your boss, maybe, if he had not died?"

"Yes, you are right. Everyone was certain he would get the deputy headmaster position."

"How did you feel about that, Zebediah? Were you angry? Jealous, maybe?"

"Never! He deserved the position. He had very good qualifications. He had even done extra teaching studies by correspondence through the church in America. But my time will come."

"But now that he is deceased, maybe your time has come sooner than you expected?"

"We shall see. No one can know. It is up to the school board in America to decide."

"Yes, yes, but you see, Zebediah, it makes you a strong suspect if his death was a murder."

"Murder? What do you mean, murder? Gideon was not murdered. I was told he was killed by an animal, a warthog."

"Maybe, maybe not. Have you ever seen a warthog in these parts?"

"No," and Zebediah's eyebrows crinkled in thought, "you are right. Not around here. In Buhera, where I come from, there are many. And they are fairly timid animals."

"And have you ever known anyone to be killed by one?"

Zebediah shook his head slowly. Sadly. And then he said, "But if Gideon's death *was* a murder, then I know who may have killed him."

Samuel looked up sharply. At last this case was beginning to move. "Who?"

"There is a night-watchman at the school complex – his name is Lucas - you should look into that man. He did not like Gideon."

"Why? Was there trouble between them?"

"Big trouble, sir. Lucas has a grand-daughter. Her name is Chastity or something like that."

"Go on," Samuel pressed, quite amazed at this man's simple-mindedness. Chastity! For God's sake!

"The old man believed that his grand-daughter had lost her virgin to Gideon."

"Lost her virgin? You mean virginity?"

"Exactly that!"

"But she is so young. When was this supposed to have happened?"

"Last year. But she is not so young. She was old enough to get pregnant."

"Pregnant? Good God, are you sure? By Gideon?"

"That is what some people are saying. But she is no longer pregnant. She lost the baby even before her belly could grow big."

§

Samuel slept soundly in his hospital bed, aided no doubt by Sister Lydia's little white pills. He had much grist for his notebook mill, and couldn't wait to get back home to write up all he had heard. As he nodded off his mind was filled with images of warthogs rooting in the muddy bank of a slow-moving river, while on a sand-bank, a crocodile was sunning itself.

§

The next morning, as dawn was breaking, Sister Lydia walked in to wake Samuel, bringing a fresh supply of the little white pills that had worked so effectively the previous afternoon, together with a bowl of hot *sadza* with some milk and sugar, and a mug of tea.

"And how do we feel today?" she asked breezily.

Samuel, his eyes still a little bleary from sleep, stretched his back out and felt a stiffness that had not been there the day before. "We feel A-OK," he lied, "couldn't be better. If you could just tell me where the bathroom is, please. I need to go."

"I can bring you a chamber-pot," said the good sister.

"No, I will go. And I need to wash as well. Can I have a towel, please sister?"

"Now, Samuel," Lydia said, consulting her wooden clip-board, "we have you scheduled for an X-ray at nine o'clock this morning. Why don't you rather wait until after your X-rays before taking a shower? If the X-rays show that everything is fine, we will discharge you and you will be free to go."

The X-Ray machine was as modern as they get. American mission hospitals tend always to have the very best. The technician took four exposures, with Dr. Jefferson, his hair shining under the radiography room lights, directing operations from inside what appeared to be a concrete bunker, with thick-glassed slits like crossbow crenellations in a castle wall.

A little while later, Jefferson came through to Samuel's ward and pronounced himself happy with the results. "Good, good," he said, squinting at the grey areas on the dark celluloid pages, "no obvious fractures, looks really good."

After a long hot shower, feeling fresh as a daisy, and stiff as a board, Samuel began to get dressed. He had to sit down on a chair in order to put his pants on, his back was that painful. His socks were an even bigger problem, but he finally managed even those.

Sister Lydia came in after he had finished dressing. "So," she said, "ready to go, are we?"

"Yes. And I must say a big thank-you for all your kindness, and of course please pass on my thanks to Doctor Jefferson as well."

"We are all just trying to be good Samaritans, like the Holy Book says."

"Before I go, sister, I heard something strange yesterday afternoon during one of my interviews. It concerned old Lucas the night-watchman and his grand-daughter Charity."

"What was it?"

"That she and Gideon may have been lovers."

A look of intense discomfort came over Sister Lydia. She lowered her eyes to her smartly polished black shoes.

"And that she may even have been pregnant?"

"I know nothing of this." She said brusquely, and immediately did an about-turn and left the room.

If Samuel had ever read Shakespeare, which he had not, he would have muttered, *'methinks she doth protest too much.'* Or perhaps the *IsiNdebele* equivalent thereof.

§

Kick-starting a Royal Enfield is a thankless task at the best of times. When the carburettor intake is full of sand and grass, it is even more difficult. But when your back feels like you have been through a laundry-mangle, your difficulties become almost impossible. Samuel had had some experience cleaning out the Indian carburettor and fortunately the Royal Enfield' apparatus was not dissimilar. Finally, having put everything back together and with a formerly clean handkerchief that now reeked of petrol, he tried to start the bike again. The magic pills seemed to have begun taking effect, so he was able to attack the kick-start with gusto. Finally the big, two-piston engine came to life, and after a couple of twists of the throttle he gingerly threw his right leg over the saddle and rode slowly away along the dirt track in the direction of the Penhalonga road. Not surprisingly he had become much more observant of the deep drifts of sand in his path.

He rode carefully along, dropping in at Mrs. Pennefather's homestead along the way to thank her again for her help in getting him to the mission hospital. He wouldn't tell her yet how profitable his stay had been.

The old lady insisted that Samuel take a wooden tray of fruit with him when he left; a half-dozen luscious kidney mangoes, the kind whose hairs never get caught in one's teeth, navel oranges, sweet tangerines, Oom Sarel yellow cling peaches and avocado pears with the consistency and taste of creamy butter. Her fifteen acres was a mini-paradise. Her husband, the late colonel, had been an expert agronomist, and the results of his years of labour were everywhere in evidence. It also helped that the property sat squarely atop an artesian well. The water it provided was sweet and plentiful even when the nearby Odzi River had been reduced to a few green puddles in a drought year.

As he arrived back at the mine-site, Samuel realised that it would behove him to go first to see Agnes rather than going straight to his office. He rode through the mine entrance, bypassing the offices and heading down the hill to his cottage. Agnes would be worried, although he knew she had been given the message about his accident and subsequent overnight stay in hospital.

She must have heard the motorcycle; she was standing on their small verandah, hands on her wide hips, a broad smile on her round face.

"That motorbike!" she said, "I should set it on fire. It is a dangerous beast!" And then she ran forward and held her man in her arms.

"Are you okay, my love? Where are you sore?"

"Everywhere. Here, here and especially here," and Samuel grabbed his lower back. "But they gave me some excellent *mushonga* -medicine, and right now I am feeling fine." He took the tray of fruit from the pillion and handed it to Agnes. "This is from Mrs. Pennefather, who saved my life." And, seeing how puzzled his wife looked, said "It's a long story, I'll tell you tonight."

§

Later that morning when Samuel finally arrived at the mine administration complex, Eddie was at his office desk poring over production numbers and shift boss reports.

"So," he said when he saw Samuel gingerly climbing the stairs to the long verandah outside his office. He had a broad grin on his face, "How's the invalid? And, more importantly, how's my bloody motor-cycle?"

"Fine and fine. Boss, we need to talk about Revue. Mr. Schwartz will be getting back either today or tomorrow and I have a gut feeling that he and his team will start milling their lunchbox ore on Sunday during the graveyard shift. That cherry-picked ore-pile is too high for them to go on much longer. When that old two-stamper fly-wheel starts turning we must be ready to catch them. And we must apprehend them with amalgam because anything else is not considered a crime."

"Hmmm." Eddie was thinking. "What about the police? Did you arrange anything with them?"

"Yes, I have. I hope you don't mind, but I offered a bed in your house to Trooper Barry Simcoe. He's been appointed by Super Thorneycroft to be our liaison. It will be him making the formal arrests, if it comes to that."

"Good. And no, not a problem about the bed, I'll tell Bella when I see her at lunchtime. When does he arrive?"

"I told him to come on Saturday afternoon, just in case Schwartz decides to get started sooner."

"Good thinking, Samuel." Eddie grinned mischievously. He was starting to get into the spirit of the adventure that seemed to be just a day or so away.

After leaving his boss, Samuel went into his small office, sat down at his desk and began to edit the detailed operational plan for what he had dubbed "The Revue Exercise."

Oh yes, The First Battalion KAR training officers in East Africa had taught him well!

Chapter 11

"Samuel!" It was Eddie, calling from his office. It sounded urgent.

"*Inkosi?*" Samuel was a little breathless from speed walking the eighty yards from the laboratory. He had been getting a crash course in amalgam treatment from one of the laboratory assistants.

"I've just received a phonogram from Umtali Post Office. Blackie Schwartz will be arriving on the 4.32 from Salisbury this afternoon. He wants to know if I will meet him at the station. Samuel, the game's afoot, as Sherlock Holmes would have said!"

"Huh?" responded Samuel who had read every Sherlock Holmes book published up to that date but couldn't remember having read that particular epithet. But Conan-Doyle's' books were a thing of the past, of that magnificent private library in the chateau near Arras. Now his reading was limited to the Illustrated London News, which he had learnt to devour weekly in France, a tattered copy of E.M.Forster's *Howard's End*, which Bella had lent him, and the odd copy of the Umtali Post that might occasionally be left in the men's change-room toilet.

§

By the time Eddie left for Umtali to collect Blackie Schwartz in his flat-bed Model T Ford that afternoon, he and Samuel had agreed upon a master plan based upon Samuel's detailed outline, together with several back-up plans should the main plan be compromised.

As Eddie's vehicle left the mine-site, Samuel went back to his office and began writing up his notes on the Warthog Tusk case. He was well-pleased with the way things were starting to develop. The potential involvement of old Lucas was somewhat disconcerting, though. Samuel had effectively dismissed the old man as a suspect despite the fact it was he who had found the body. He had considered the man to be physically incapable of the murder. His fingers were horribly misshapen, and Samuel had first-hand experience of the speed at which the old man walked. And yet. And yet. Always the 'and yet' when love and family honour is involved. He decided he needed to talk to Charity.

Soon. Alone.

§

Early the next morning, Saturday, Samuel rode the Royal Enfield over to Eddie and Bella's house and, hearing noises in the kitchen area, knocked on the front door.

126

"Hello, Samuel," said Bella, looking quite radiant in her seventh month of pregnancy. "How are you feeling after your tumble? Mrs. Pennefather was around here yesterday for afternoon tea. She thought you were a goner." Bella and the old lady were very close. When Bella had first arrived in Penhalonga as a teacher she had boarded with the Pennefather's, and only left them once she married Eddie.

"I am fine now Missus," Samuel replied, "but when she found me, I also thought I was a goner. Miss Bella, is Boss Eddie here?"

Eddie came through at his wife's summoning, surprised to see Samuel up and about so early.

"Yes," he answered to Samuel's questioning, "I dropped Blackie Schwartz at the Revue mine-site at about seven o'clock last evening. He has no idea we know of his involvement, of that I am certain."
"Good, that's a relief. I was worried about that. We need them to start milling without looking over their shoulders."

"Yes. Now your plan called for an informer to be there on the ground to give the signal when the milling starts. What have you done about that? And won't they be suspicious if they see some stranger hanging around the old mill?"

"Not this particular stranger." Samuel then told Eddie about the young herd-boy who had retrieved his motor-cycle from the long grass.

"I have promised him ten shillings if everything goes according to plan. His cover will be that he is looking for a stray calf around the bone-yard. He is only eleven or twelve years old, so I'm sure they will ignore him. He will know where we are concealed and will warn us once the milling has started. I am on my way to Old Umtali mission to pick him up right now."

After Samuel had left, having politely refused Bella's offer of a hot cup of sweetened tea, Eddie turned to his wife and said, "What a man! He always seems to come up with a plan that just amazes me. Imagine that, Bella! Using a young herd-boy as an infiltrator. Bloody clever!"

§

Farai was the young lad's name. Farai Bere. The root of his first name translates as 'happy', but this young man was anything but happy. He had a very serious look on his face.

"You look scared, Farai," said Samuel when, as arranged, he met him at the main road entrance to the Old Umtali mission.

"No, *baba*, not scared. I just want to make sure that I earn that money you promised me. Ten shillings, remember?"

Samuel reassured him of their agreement then showed him how to swing his leg over the pillion seat and told him to put his arms around Samuel's waist and hang on tight.

Less than a half-hour later, Samuel pulled up in front of his mine house in a cloud of dust. Agnes came out to greet them.

"You must be Farai?" she said. "Are you hungry? Come inside."

She had made a pot of tea, and poured an enamel mug, sweetening it with a healthy dollop of condensed milk from a Carnation can. Then she cut a thick wedge of brown bread, spreading it liberally with butter and apricot jam. Farai's eyes were as wide as saucers as he began his meal. From the look of his bony physique it appeared that he didn't often enjoy a meal of such substance.

Later, Samuel took Farai up to the mine-site, much quieter now that it was a Saturday, and showed him around. The young boy seemed particularly interested in the mill room, as noisy as it was.

Agnes had made a bed for Farai in Hastings' room. He would be staying for two nights, although Samuel had no idea what time they would be returning on Sunday evening. It would all depend on how things developed at Revue. He was now not even sure that *anything* would happen. He just had a hunch, and sometimes hunches have a habit of back-firing. Anyway, he thought, it will be worth the ten shillings just to keep an eye on Blackie and his thieving chums.

"Come, Farai, let's go and earn your money." Samuel wanted to go and do a 'recce' at Revue. It was only about a twenty minute ride away, so he told Agnes, "we'll be back before supper."

§

Samuel dropped Farai off along the main road running past Revue mine, pointing out carefully through the leaves of the trees where the bone-yard was situated. The boy nodded his understanding and, grasping his herding stick with its long leather thong, moved off like a wraith through the brush. In minutes he had disappeared from sight, his drab, ragged clothing blending in perfectly with the thick scrub.

Samuel had found a thick area of grass near a wild-fig tree. He laid the bike down and covered it with a few tufts of grass, then moved twenty yards away to view the results. With its olive-green colour, one would have to walk over the bike before it could actually be seen. He then settled down under the fig-tree, its large leaves providing excellent protection against the fierce late-afternoon sun. Up above bees buzzed busily as they feasted on the sweetness of the ripening figs. Once the diurnal bees had returned to their hives it would be the turn of the nocturnal fruit-bats.

The steady clanking of the Revue four-stamp mill in the middle distance was hypnotic and soon Samuel began to doze, his aching back propped up against the huge, smooth, multi-faceted trunk of the fig tree. Suddenly he sensed a presence next to him and he awoke with a start.

"Baba," said Farai, "It is I."

"Mukomana. Sit down with me. Tell me what you saw."

The young lad crouched down on his haunches. He seemed to have entered into the exercise with a spirit of adventure, a Kiplingesque Kim to Samuel's Colonel Creighton, and was anxious to report his findings.

"I walked all around that place you call the bone-yard, but I saw no bones, only parts of machinery overgrown with grass and vines and small saplings. Then I saw some men arrive and do something at the noisy house. It was like they were turning on a tap. And then the big wheel on that tall machine started to turn and make a big noise. After five minutes, one of the men ran back to the tap and turned it off and the wheel slowly stopped turning. From what I could hear, they just seemed to be testing it."

"Good, good. You are a very good spy, Farai."

Everything that Farai had reported could well have been expected to happen.

"Did you by any chance see a pile of whitish-looking rock nearby?"

"Oh yes, quite near the big machine. It was about as high as a big bull," Farai held up his arm above his head, "and *this* long," and he paced out a distance of thirty feet. "As they left, one of them said, 'see you this time tomorrow'.

§

Agnes had cooked a delicious meal of roast chicken. There were a few customers for her beer who could not or possibly would not, pay cash, providing instead chickens, ears of maize, sweet-melons and other delectable foodstuffs in exchange. To Agnes it didn't matter. Her family had to eat, and bartering was a good way to cut out the retailing middle man.

Young Farai ate with gusto, and Agnes wondered when last the boy had had a decent meal. Field mice and small birds are no substitute for roast chicken.

131

"Where are you from, Farai?" she asked him, "where is your *musha*?"

"My family is from Inyanga, but they are all gone. After my grandparents died, my mother came to work at the mission as a cleaner, but then she also got sick. It was Flu. She died three months ago." Farai began to snuffle.

"There, there, my boy, don't be sad." Agnes rubbed his shoulders motheringly. "What about your father? Where is he?"

"He went to work in Jo'burg, on the mines. He went two years ago. We never heard from him again."

Agnes patted his head. "Hau, you have lived a tough life for one so young."

"It's not too bad, *amai*, I have employment as a herder at the mission. They give me food from time to time and a hut to sleep in, and sometimes they give me old clothes."

"And school? Do you go to school?"

"No, *amai*, I have never been to school."

Agnes looked at her husband, who up until now had been a mere bystander in this two-way conversation.

"Samuel, this is not right. An eleven year-old boy who has never been to school? And, on top of it, he is employed by the mission which has an elementary school? Hau!" The Hau! was said more out of disgust than amazement.

She looked Samuel squarely in the eye. "Do you think Missus Evans would take him into her school?"

"I can ask. But where would he stay, Agnes? He has no family here in Penhalonga."

"He can stay with us. We can be his family."

Samuel just looked at his wife, wordless, wondering how on earth a man could be so lucky to have such a woman for a wife.

Chapter 12

This was the day. This *has* to be the day, thought Samuel.

"Farai! Get up you lazy boy, get up!" But when he looked into Hastings' room, Farai's woven grass sleeping pallet was neatly rolled and the blankets that Agnes had given him were precisely folded and placed against the wall. But Farai was nowhere to be seen.

Concerned, Samuel went into the kitchen where he could hear Agnes working, tin plates and pots clanging as she prepared their breakfast.

"Have you seen Farai?" he asked her.

"Oh yes, he was up long before you, my husband. He must have heard me in the kitchen. We talked for quite a while about whether I had been serious about him moving here with us. I think he was quite moved. He is so alone Samuel."

"I know, I know. So where is he now?"

"I sent him with a pail of beer to my father's house. He should be back any minute."

It will be interesting to hear what Amos thinks of the young boy, thought Samuel.

And then along came the subject of his thoughts, barefoot and with nothing but a loin-cloth about his waist, swinging an empty enamel pail and whistling a tune which Samuel recognized from wild parties in Agnes' shebeen in the months before he had left for the war. He wondered if Farai knew the words that went along with the tune. They were very rude, and certainly not something that an eleven-year old boy should know.

They went something like:

Iwe Lucia, amaiwaco wano dada,
Hey you, Lucy, your mother's very snooty
Aio mahobo, handakakuchengatera
Please keep your maidenhead for me.

§

After breakfast, Samuel fired up the Royal Enfield and with Farai clinging on behind him, took the road from the mine to Eddie's house in the village. They were expected, for Eddie was sitting out on the shaded verandah smoking a cigarette.

"Samuel, top of the morning to you," he greeted. "And who is this young man you have with you?"

"This is Farai. Farai, please greet Mister Evans. He is the big boss."

Farai clapped his hands together politely and murmured, "*Mangwanani, Ishe.*"

"*Mangwanani*, Farai. So, Samuel, bring me up to date. What happened last evening?"

Samuel described the events of the previous day, not diminishing in any way the good work done by Farai. Eddie seemed genuinely impressed.

"Well done, Farai," he said in Chishona. "You have earned your pay." And he pulled his wallet out of his pocket. "Do you want paper money or gold?"

"I was promised four half-crowns, so that is what I want; four silver half crowns."

Samuel and Eddie laughed loudly.

"They are the same thing, Farai. But you are right. If you were promised silver coins, then silver it shall be." And Eddie took out his purse and scrabbled for four half-crowns."

Eddie turned to Samuel. "So are we still on for this evening? Your friend Simcoe is here, still asleep I should imagine. We sank quite a few whiskies last night."

"Yes. I am more convinced than ever they will start milling this afternoon. To be absolutely sure, we should have Farai go in again and send a signal."

"Quite right, if he's prepared to do it." Eddie turned towards the young lad. "Want to do it all again, Farai? Tonight? Same money?" Farai nodded his head rapidly.

"I knew he would agree; he seems to have a very entrepreneurial spirit!" said Samuel, a big grin on his face.

Bella came out to say hello, followed shortly thereafter by Barry Simcoe, his short blond hair tussled by sleep, and his eyes red and hurting. That'll teach you for trying to go one-on-one with Eddie Evans, thought Samuel.

"Miss Bella?"

"Yes, Samuel?"

"Agnes was wondering if you would be able to take on another student at you school. He is eleven and has never even had one day of schooling in his life."

Bella looked at Farai. She knew exactly to whom Samuel was referring.

"Yes, I think so, Samuel. It would be a challenge, but I think it can be done. Where would he stay?"

"Agnes says that if you will teach him, we will house him."

"That's a huge responsibility, Samuel. Where is his own family? Would they agree to this?"

"His family is dead. Well, not quite. He has a father who went to work on the mines in *Egoli*." Samuel used the local nickname for Johannesburg which literally means 'The Gold'.

"When did the father go?"

"Two years ago and he and his mother have heard nothing from him since he left."

"Mother? But you said he had no family."

"The mother caught Spanish Flu last year. She is now deceased."

"Oh, you poor boy," said Bella, looking at Farai with pity. Farai, for his part, had no idea what they were saying, only that he was the subject of their conversation.

§

And now it was four o'clock and the worst of the afternoon heat had abated. Samuel and Farai parked the Royal Enfield under the same wild fig tree where they had parked the previous day. Eddie and Barry had travelled together in the flatbed Model T and were parked in a narrow side lane, well hidden from any traffic passing on the main road.

Farai went off in his herd-boy guise. Samuel glanced at his watch and couldn't help thinking of his old pal. Hastings, he thought, if only you could be here now, we'd have such fun together arresting these black-hearted *mbavha*.

And then Samuel heard the hiss of steam and the clanking of the old two-stamp mill began. Farai came scooting back through the bushes.

"They are starting to shovel the rocks into the big machine," he said, breathlessly. "Is this what you have been waiting for?"

"Yes. Is the white boss there? Yes? Good. Come with me."

138

They ran to where Eddie and Barry were parked. Samuel crouched by the driver-side window.

"It has begun, *Inkosi*. Let us not be too hasty. Remember we need them to have the amalgam in their possession for the arrest to be a good one. And the best thing of all, Blackie Schwartz is with them."

"Right," said Eddie. "How long do you think we should wait before we call the cavalry?"

"Huh?" asked Samuel. Cavalry? What was this man talking about? The only cavalry he had ever come across had been in Flanders in 1915 and they hadn't lasted long against the big chattering German machine guns.

"Forget it," said Eddie, smiling to himself, and starting up the Model T. "Want a ride?" he asked, gesturing towards the flat bed behind him.

"No," said Samuel emphatically, "we must stick to the plan. I will cut across through the bush and stand by as a stopping force. You and Simcoe go around by road."

Samuel and Farai ran back through the now darkening bush. When they arrived at the fig tree, an easy point of reference against the skyline, Farai took Samuel's hand and whispered, "Follow me. It is this way."

Samuel was convinced Farai had the eyes of a leopard. He led them straight to the stamp mill like a moth to a flame. They stopped on the fringe of the bush, knowing that they could not be seen against the darkness of the trees.

Schwartz' men had strung up a weak overhead light and under its pale yellow beam four men toiled shovelling chunks of pale white quartz into the old two-stamp mill. Schwartz himself was busy at the mill's outlet, overseeing the amalgamating process as the finely ground slurry slowly oozed over copper plates coated with mercury.

As Samuel watched Schwartz, the big man suddenly looked up, an amalgam plate in his hands. He had heard his name but couldn't see the two men coming out of the light. Within seconds Simcoe had Schwartz' hands behind his back and was putting on heavy steel handcuffs. Blackie's men continued to shovel on; because of the loud clanking of the mill, they were oblivious to what had happened to their Fagin.

Samuel walked out of the shadows, and with his old and trusty *knobkerrie* raised and with Eddie and Barry Simcoe coming from behind, all four raised their hands in surrender. They had them all!

"Now what did the plan say we would do with them?" asked Eddie. "I want the milling to continue, this is really high grade ore they're processing."

"Whatever you do," said Samuel, "please, I beg of you, do *not* put them in a disused boiler." Remembering so clearly the fate of Justice Sibanda almost five years earlier, they both laughed uproariously until tears poured from their eyes. Simcoe and Farai just looked confused. Oh yes, it was an inside joke, all right!

§

It was well past midnight when the last of the pilfered, cherry-picked ore had been processed and Eddie had removed the amalgam from the copper plates. His experience told him that this was a rich haul, probably the richest one day result in the mine's four year history.

§

As they drove through the gates of the Umtali police camp early the next morning, curious off-duty policemen milled about wondering what this was all about – a white man in handcuffs chained up with four black labourers like some common criminal? This sort of thing just didn't happen in 1919 Rhodesia. Scandalous! There would be many whispered conversations that night in the hallowed salons of the Umtali Club.

Simcoe had prepared the formal charges with the help of the public prosecutor and it was expected that the case could come to trial within three months. Eddie and Samuel spent the entire day going over their statements with the prosecutor, a process they both found extremely tedious.

Under tough police questioning, the four labourers gave up another six mine-workers who were in on the scheme. They had quickly established that Frikkie Meyer was *not* involved in the cherry-picking venture, much to Eddie's dismay, but they still needed to complete the chain of gold-selling. Blackie was a king-pin, yes, but there had to be someone who was *buying* the gold, and Blackie's mouth was sealed tighter than a clam.

As Eddie had suspected, the thievery had started soon after the start-up of the mine. Blackie Schwartz had realized that the mine was a lot richer than the original mine-owner had suspected, and had been cherry-picking the best-looking ore for separate processing almost from the outset. The death of the owner in the muddy trenches of France had been a boon for Blackie because the widow had no-one else to rely on, and had accepted his word as gospel.

Eddie, too, had been duped. Under normal circumstances he may not even have bought the supposedly marginal mine, but he had felt very sorry for the widow and wanted to liberate her from the financial burden to which she was captive, as well as free her of the worry of running a gold-mine with all its attendant administrative complexities. And with his blind trust in Blackie Schwartz he had not seen the cherry-picking going on under his very nose. No, for that he had to thank Samuel. And, of course, young Farai, who was now the proud owner of *eight* silver half-crowns. Nine if you included the one Samuel had given him for his motor-cycle retrieval services.

And of course there was Agnes, whose potent brew had unleashed those loose tongues at the wedding feast.

Chapter 13

"Farai!"

"Farai, *muka iwe*" There was no response from the room where Farai slept. Agnes looked at the kitchen clock, a wind-up affair, much louder than it was accurate, with two silver alarm bells on top. Nine o'clock! It was late. Yes, she knew he had only got back from Revue somewhat after two o'clock in the morning, but this was ridiculous.

"Farai!" Exasperated, Agnes opened the bedroom door. The room was empty, the bedclothes neatly folded and placed on a chair. Surely he hadn't gone in to Umtali with Eddie and Samuel and the Revue prisoners? That was never the plan, yet where could the young boy be?

And then she saw the note that Samuel had left for her. It was held in place by the alarm clock.

My dear wife (the note read),

Farai is with us. Mr. Evans has made arrangements for him to begin his schooling today at Missus Bella's school in Penhalonga. He will go home with Missus Bella after school, and she will give him extra teaching at her home. I will bring him home in time for supper.

With all my great affection, your husband, Samuel

That evening, the newly enlarged family of four sat around their small dining room table sharing a meal of steaming *sadza*, together with a stew of short ribs, flavoured with a pod of red chili pepper. Vegetables comprised fresh green kale which Agnes grew in the plot of land behind their house, and carrots, cut into thick medallions, like golden coins. There was milk for the two boys and a foaming enamel mug of Agnes' best *hwahwa* beer for Samuel.

"So, Farai, I missed you today," said Agnes. "What did you learn?"

"At school I learnt so many things. First, I learnt how to write the letters A to K. Then I learnt how to add up and take-away numbers. Then I learnt how stupid my fellow-students were. Hau! Those boys know nothing. I asked one boy of my age what he would do if a calf became trapped in the mud by the side of a river after the rains. He did not know! Can you believe it? Hau!" And he shook his head in disbelief. But he was not done yet.

"And then Missus Bella took me back to her house and I had more lessons. She read from a very old black book, and then asked me many questions afterwards to see if I understood what she had read to me."

"And what book was this? A history book?"

"No, history came later. This was a book about a man and a woman living in a garden just like Mrs. Pennefather's, with much fruits and vegetables. The garden's name was Eden. But even with such a rich garden, the man and woman were very, very poor, even poorer than me."

"Why do you say that, Farai?"

"Well, I saw a picture in that book, and these two, the man and the woman, they were naked, they had no clothes!"

Agnes and Samuel laughed until the tears ran down their faces. Even little Hastings joined in, although he wasn't really quite sure what the joke was about.

§

The next morning Samuel rode the Royal Enfield up to the mine offices. He wanted to see Eddie, not only to chat about the events of last Sunday evening, but also to discuss implementing procedures that would help them avoid the same kind of fraud happening in the future – at Revue, Rezende, and any other mine that Eddie might own in the future.

It was past nine when Eddie strolled into his office. By the long white jacket he was wearing, Samuel surmised that Eddie had just returned from the laboratory.

"Did you get a final reading on Sunday night's milling at Revue?" he asked.

"Yes," Eddie replied, "actually, that's where I've just come from. It was outstanding! Nothing less. We netted one hundred and seventy-three ounces grading at around ninety-four percent pure. If you do the math, that material that Blackie and his boys cherry-picked was running at right around ten ounces per ton of ore. Spectacular!"

They chatted a little about the unqualified success of the operation, and also about what demands would be placed on their respective time as the case against Blackie Schwartz and his men made its lugubrious way through the legal system.

Finally, Samuel broached the subject of Gideon Munyaradzi.

"Boss Eddie. I need a little time to attend to that other problem, the warthog murder. I know you said to take whatever time I needed, but I just wanted to clear it with you. That way, if you don't see me for a few days you will not think that I am slacking."

"I would never think that, Samuel. No, you go and do what you have to do. Is there anything I can help you with?"

"Not yet, it is still too early. I have so many thoughts going on in my brain, at least two, maybe three suspects, but how, always the question *how* was it done? And, even more important, why? Always the same question: what was the motive?"

§

Samuel left Eddie in his office and headed up the road towards Old Umtali and the Methodist Mission. There were some people he wanted to chat to. After that, he planned on riding into Umtali to spend some time with Simcoe. Last Sunday Barry had mentioned that he had some information regarding potassium cyanide, but things had become too hectic for them to take the discussion any further.

Samuel was met at the night-watchman's house by Charity who was hanging some washing on the line. Her grandfather was still sleeping, she informed Samuel, and would only awaken at about three or four o'clock that afternoon. If Samuel needed to talk to Lucas he would have to wait: she would not awaken the old man too early; he needed his rest.

"No, Charity, it is you I wish to speak with," said Samuel. "You have not been open with me. You kept information from me, and that always makes me very suspicious." Samuel's face had become hard and cold, devoid of any emotion.

"Information?" She seemed incredulous. "I don't know what you mean. I answered all your questions truthfully."

"Perhaps. But you never told me that you and Gideon had been lovers. Or that you had become pregnant by him. These are very important things for an investigator to know, Charity. We are not playing children's games, you know. There is a man who is dead and I need *all* the information surrounding his death that it is possible to find out. So, is it true?"

Samuel could see that his harsh words, delivered without any pretense of gentleness, had had the desired effect. The young woman, for that was truly what she was, a woman, not a young girl as Samuel had at first regarded her, began to cry. There was no sobbing, but huge tears rolled down her cheeks and darkened the bodice of her light blue dress.

"Yes," she began, "Gideon was my first and only love. I loved him from the first time I saw him when I was in standard four. He was my teacher. Then in my last year of elementary school I let him know of my love for him. I sent him letters, love letters; silly, childish, girlish love letters. But he ignored them. For nearly two years he ignored my obvious love for him. But then, in my last week of elementary school I told him that if he did not meet me that evening at the *kopje,* I would hang myself from the iron tree that grows beside the giant boulder there.

"I had been there for fifteen minutes before he arrived. At first he was very angry with me. He told me that such love liaisons between teacher and student were forbidden, taboo, that he could lose his job even if we were *seen* together outside of the classroom. But I pressed myself upon him; I don't know what had come over me. It was lust that filled me that evening and I forced him to make love to me."

"But that must have been over a year ago, so you were what, fourteen?"

"Yes, fourteen, and he was twenty-three. Oh and how we loved each other. After the first time, we met there every night for a week until school broke up and he went to one of the other missions to receive higher education."

"And that's when you became pregnant?"

"No, not then. It was about six months later when I came back from Sakubva to visit my grandfather. I had not seen Gideon for all that time. I seduced him in his room one night while he was sleeping."

"And I understand you lost the baby?"

"You can say 'lost', but it was intentional."

"You had an abortion? Good God! Surely you know that abortions are illegal. Who performed the operation?"

"You may say that abortions are illegal, but it may surprise you to learn that there are many such operations performed every day in this country. Certain ladies have the knowledge of which herbs and bulbs and roots to mix to make a soup which will result in a miscarriage."

"And that's what happened to you? Who was this lady?"

"I have told you enough, Mr. Kumalo. Please let me get on with my house-keeping."

This was all great information about the deceased, thought Samuel, but it had done nothing to add a suspect to his short list. Yes, if the grandfather had discovered the secret of Charity's deflowering and later pregnancy, that was certainly motive enough to kill Gideon. But old Lucas just didn't strike Samuel as the killer type. No, I'd better keep on investigating, he thought.

And the mantra of 'motive' kept swirling in his head.

§

"Good morning, Mister Sykes," greeted Samuel, knocking politely on the half-open door of the headmaster's office.

"Mr. Kumalo! Good morning, your ears must be burning."

149

Samuel put a hand up to one of his ears, looking a little puzzled. "I don't understand," he said.

"No, no, I'm sorry, it's just a saying that one says when you've been talking about someone and that person then appears."

"Aha. And you were talking about me?"

"Yes. I had Doctor Jefferson up here earlier this morning to talk about hospital matters. He told me that you had been an overnight patient of his late last week."

"Yes," said Samuel, shuffling his feet, a little embarrassed. "I fell off my motor-cycle, slid on some sand. I was going much too fast for the conditions."

"Anyway, he said that you had made a good, swift recovery."

"Very much so, thanks to excellent medical attention from both Doctor Jefferson and Sister Lydia Mukarakate. And of course we must not forget that modern invention, the X-Ray machine."

"Yes, our congregation in Dallas is so very good to us when it comes to hospital supplies and equipment. Very generous indeed. Not so generous unfortunately when it comes to teaching supplies." Mr. Sykes sounded somewhat querulous. Samuel suspected there might exist a certain degree of rivalry between the two branches of the mission station. Especially when it came to scarce resources.

"Mr. Sykes, I'm sorry to have to take up your time again, but I have more questions with respect to the Gideon affair."

"Well, God bless my soul, Mistuh Kumalo, I cannot believe how much time and effort y'all are putting into an accidental death. Surely you have other, more important things to do?"

"I am representing his mother, a poor widow, who is not convinced that his death *was* an accident." Samuel was stretching the truth a little here: Gideon's mother had no idea that her son's case had been officially escalated to murder, nor even that it was being investigated. He still had to sit down with the old lady and gently break the news to her. He made a mental note to ask Agnes to help him with *that* particular task.

"How on earth could it possibly be anything but an accident?" The look on Mr. Sykes' face showed genuine surprise.

"That is exactly what I am investigating. Now Mr. Sykes, did you know of the romantic relationship between Gideon and Charity, your night-watchman's granddaughter?"

Sykes looked utterly shocked and Samuel believed that this information was a total bombshell for the school principal.

"Gideon and Charity? Involved romantically? I find that very difficult to believe. Good God, man, he was, what eight years older than her?"

"Nine, actually."

151

"When did the relationship start? Was it while he was her teacher? Here, at Old Umtali?"

"No. It was in the month of holidays before she started high school in Sakubva."

"Praise be to God! I mean if it's true that one of my teachers had an affair with a high-school student, that's bad enough, terrible, actually. But if she had been his pupil at the time, oh my, what a scandal!"

"She became pregnant by him too. Had an abortion or somehow induced a miscarriage, possibly with the use of herbs and so on."

Now Sykes was almost apoplectic, his face red with anger. "Oh, how could someone do that? I can forgive the affair, forgive the getting pregnant, but murdering an unborn child? That is something I just cannot condone! It runs against all of my church's Christian principles."

"Mr. Sykes, please remember that none of this has been proven, it is all just hearsay and conjecture." Samuel was lying, for Charity had herself told him of the pregnancy and abortion, but he got the feeling that Sykes was ready to banish Lucas and his granddaughter from the mission, and where was the sense in that? The old man was so riddled with arthritis he would never be able to find another job.

"Please don't rush to judgement, Mr. Sykes. Now, sir, I was wondering if I could have a look at Gideon's room."

"You can certainly look at his room, but you won't find anything. Everything was cleared out and boxed up over a week ago."

"And the boxes? Where are they?"

"I believe they were sent to his mother in Penhalonga."

Samuel made a quick entry in his note-book.

"Mr. Sykes, your colleague, Dr. Jefferson? How long has he been here at the Old Umtali mission hospital?"

Sykes looked heavenward for guidance. "Hmmm, let's see now. I guess it would be just nigh on a year. Yep, that's right, just gone a year."

"And Sister Mukarakate?"

"Oh, I can't really say for sure, but she was working at the hospital when I arrived, and that's just over three years ago."

"What is your congregation's policy on overseas placements?" Sykes looked a little bewildered at the question. "I mean, how long would you normally expect to stay before heading back home?"

"Ah, I see. Normally, depending on the circumstances, an overseas posting is for approximately three years. Then a two year posting within the USA and then off again to one of our other overseas missions for another three years."

"So Doctor Jefferson is likely to be here for another two years or so?"

153

"With medical people it's a little different. There could be some specialist training course that comes up that he applies for and is selected to attend, and then his posting could be shorter."

"What kind of training?"

"Well, let's say, for example, Dr. Jefferson is a general practitioner and wants to specialize in cardiology. See what I mean?"

Samuel was nodding his head.

"What specialities does Doctor Jefferson have already, do you know?"

"Well I know that to qualify for a posting to a mission station hospital such as this, he must have done extensive training in tropical diseases and also obstetrics and gynecology. Yes, indeed. I believe he told me that he did his OBGYN training at the medical school in Edinburgh, Scotland."

"Why not in Texas?"

"My dear man, you can't be serious! Being a black man he had to go to a university in New York just to get his basic medical training. The Civil War and slavery may have ended over fifty years ago but segregation is still alive and well in most of the southern United States, including Texas. Especially Texas."

Chapter 14

The young police cadet guarding the front gate had come to know Samuel quite well, even stood to attention when the Royal Enfield rolled up in a cloud of dust.

"*Munoda* Superintendent Thorneycroft *here*?" he queried respectfully.

"*Aiwa,* no, not today. I'm here to see Trooper Simcoe."

The big red and white striped metal boom was raised, the young cadet leaning heavily on the counterweight. "Go right on, sir, I'll phone ahead."

"Morning, Samuel, lovely day, isn't it?"

What is it with these Englishmen? thought Samuel. Why are they so fixated on the weather? Does he not know that sunny days mean no rain, and no rain means poor crops? And a poor crop means hungry children?

But all Samuel said was: "Yes, lovely. On Sunday you told me that you had some information for me concerning cyanide. We didn't have time to chat what with the Schwartz & Co. arrests going on. What can you tell me?"

Simcoe opened his notebook, flipping a few pages.

"Right. Well, I went to Daggit's, as you'd suggested. Not much there except to confirm Mr. Evans' belief that there are no gold mines in the Umtali area that use cyanide for gold extraction. There is one mine near Rusape that recently went into production and it was engineered to use cyanide from the get go. Apparently the gold is very widely disseminated and the ore-body is not very rich so they can't use mercury. And it's an open pit mine, so what they don't get in yield they make up for in throughput."

"You sound like you've learnt a lot!"

"The manager at Daggit's was very helpful; he spent a great deal of time with me. But I don't think I did more than scratch the surface."

"What's the name of the mine near Rusape?"

"Oh yes, sorry." Simcoe scrabbled through his note-book, flipping pages. "Ah yes, here we are. It's the Golden Dawn. Located north of Rusape just off the main road to Inyanga. It's only been open about three months."

"Did you ask what kind of cyanide they use?"

"Simcoe flipped pages again. "Sodium, it says here. Sodium cyanide. Does that help?"

"It's very similar to the chemical that killed Gideon, but it doesn't help that the closest possible source is a mine over sixty miles away." Samuel paused, thinking. "And what about old Mr. Mitchell at the chemist's shop? Did he give you anything?"

"I called there that same day, as you suggested, but he had gone to the Vumba for a long weekend. The lady who was in charge didn't have a clue about chemicals, just perfumes and baby powder."

Samuel laughed. "I think I know who dealt with you. Sounds like Mrs. Gaitskill. She seems like a prying old busybody at first, but she's actually a very nice, kind lady. She went out of her way to obtain a special wedding present for my late boss to give to Mr. and Mrs. Evans at their wedding. She had to order it especially from England."

"Are you talking about Hastings Follett?"

"Yes, Hastings Follett," said Samuel sadly. He often thought of his old friend and wondered what he would do in a case as bewildering as this one.

"Okay, Mr. Barry, you've been very helpful. I think I'll just go and see Mr. Mitchell myself; I've got a bit of time available. By the way, what's the latest on the Revue boys?"

"Oh, they're all pointing fingers hither and yon. The only silent one is Blackie himself. Probably because he is the only one with a lawyer. I should tell you that Mr. Thorneycroft is tickled pink with the outcome. He's been sending messages to PGHQ to the effect that the BSAP should do more of this civilian cooperation thing."

"I wonder what their response was when they found out I was involved." said Samuel, a very wry look on his face.

§

"Well, well, well, if it isn't Constable Kumalo! How have you been?" The old pharmacist seemed genuinely happy to see Samuel, pumping his hand three times in the traditional Shona way. I wonder if he even knows that I'm Matabele, not Shona, thought Samuel. And Samuel didn't have the heart to tell him he was no longer a constable.

After the obligatory small talk in Mr. Mitchell's back office/storeroom, much of it surrounding the loss to the community of Trooper Follett, Samuel was finally able to get a word in edgeways.

"I'm pursuing a line of enquiry in a case I'm assisting the police with. It relates to potassium cyanide, its availability to the general public and so on."

"Ah yes, Mrs. Gaitskill told me that there'd been a policeman in here while I was away. I wondered what it may have been about. So. Potassium cyanide, hey? It's mainly used in industrial applications, gold extraction, that sort of thing, but increasingly it's used in the manufacture of plastics and so on.
"I carry a certain amount of it here in the pharmacy, under lock and key, I might add, because it's extremely toxic, poisonous, but there is very little call for it. I keep it mainly for the schools around here. They use it from time to time in laboratory experiments."

"Can you tell me which schools have purchased any over the last, say, two years?"

"Of course. Just give me a minute; I'll need to consult my poison register." Mitchell got up and walked over to a cabinet marked "POISONS", unlocked it with a key from a chain he kept secured to his belt, and took out a black book which he brought back with him to his desk.

On its front the index book was marked:

POISON REGISTER 1917 –

in a beautiful italic script.

"We're obliged to keep this register by law. Good thing, too. As I recall, that's how your friend Follett discovered the source of the strychnine that killed that gold thief out at Rezende Mine. Oh, forgive me, Samuel. You were a part of that investigation too, weren't you? If anyone would know about it, you would."

The register showed that four schools had purchased potassium cyanide within the past two years, the Dominican Convent, Umtali Girls High School, Umtali Boys High School and Old Umtali Mission School. At Samuel's request, Mitchell produced the original purchase order from the mission school. It was dated just one month earlier and was signed by the Headmaster, Mr. Ronald W. Sykes.

Interesting, thought Samuel, very interesting. But not conclusive evidence of anything. He suspected that Sykes had merely signed the purchase order along with a dozen

159

other orders without even giving it a second glance. Then he had a brilliant thought and promptly said thank-you and farewell to the old pharmacist.

§

"Doctor Snelgar?" Samuel was knocking loudly on the medical examiner's door. No response, and yet the receptionist had said that she had not seen the doctor leave, so he *had* to be in his rooms.

Then along came the grizzled pathologist walking with a jaunty spring in his step down the corridor holding a steaming mug of tea in one hand. Samuel had walked right by the nurses' wardroom and was convinced that the door had been closed. Very unusual. Hmmm.

"So, Samuel Kumalo, what can I do for you?"

"Well, doc, I believe I have located the source of the poison that you found in Gideon."

"Ah, good. Sit down and tell me all about it."

"Well, Mitchell's Pharmacy sold a small amount, just 50 milligrams, to the Old Umtali Mission School. According to the register it was for 'laboratory and lepidoptery experiments', but then I got to thinking and decided I'd better ask someone qualified to answer the question."

"And who is that?" asked Snelgar.

"You of course, sir. The question I have is this: is chemistry taught in elementary school, or is it limited to high schools?"

160

"Well, in my day, many years ago, I should add, it was only taught starting in Senior School, Form 2, and laboratory work, experiments and so on, even later than that."

"That is exactly what I thought!"

"But, why do you ask?"

"Because the Old Umtali Mission school is only an elementary school, only goes up to standard five. After that the students are sent to other schools to learn at higher grades."

Snelgar's eyes showed surprise. Surprise mingled perhaps with a *soupcon* of admiration for the innate intelligence of this tough Matabele ex-policeman.

And then there was a gentle rap on the door.

"Graham? Graham, are you there?"

The door opened slowly, almost hesitantly, and as Samuel turned his head, there stood Connie Snyman. She was in her nurse's uniform, but that did nothing to detract from her femininity. She still wore the same short, sandy-blonde hair, the green eyes that twinkled in the bright lights of the mortuary. She was still very athletic looking, her calf muscles nicely toned from the games of tennis that she played at least three times a week at the Hillside country club.

"Samuel!" she exclaimed, a broad smile creasing her face and crinkling her eyes. "How nice to see you again! I'd heard that you were back in town, or should I say, in Penhalonga."

Samuel stood up and held out his hand. Connie would have none of a simple hand-shake, and despite her highly conservative South African background, she held out her arms for a hug.

"I'm so glad you made it back unscathed," she said. "It was a bad war. We've had quite a few men in the hospital whose bodies are healthy but whose minds are badly injured, and may never recover."

"Not like the wars of my day," said Snelgar. "At least we just used bullets and artillery shells. None of this mustard and chlorine gas that they used in France."

And of course they talked of Hastings Follett. When had Samuel last seen him? Had he been well? What were the circumstances of his death? Is it true that he had married a French woman, had had a posthumous child?

As Samuel said his goodbyes, leaving the grizzled doctor with the young, vivacious nurse, he couldn't help wondering if the two of them were romantically involved. Snelgar must be in his mid-fifties, he thought, Connie maybe twenty-five or six. But if there are no young men around, what's a young lass to do? Ah yes, Kaiser Wilhelm and his cousin King George sure had a lot to answer for. There were a lot of young men never coming home.

Chapter 15

Every Thursday evening without fail, Jock Mitchell, proprietor of Mitchell's Pharmacy, hosted a poker game at his house in Murambi, a pleasant suburb on the northern foothill slopes of Umtali. The solidly built red brick houses with tiled roofs were each surrounded by a minimum of one acre of well-watered and manicured lawns, with beds of roses, arum lilies, stralitzia, bougainvillea and a thousand and one other colourful tropical plants. Murambi was definitely *the* high-end suburb of the town.

The poker games always started promptly at seven-thirty, but Jock's guests would arrive anytime after seven for a 'wee drappie' before the game started. It seemed that, despite shortages of so many luxury items caused by the Great War that had raged for the past four years, Jock always seemed to have a way of procuring his favourite single malt scotches. No one asked how he managed it, not even Spencer Thorneycroft, who, as senior policeman in Manicaland, should have been keeping an eye out for such flagrant breeches of the rationing regulations. In theory anyway.

On this particular evening there were only four players in attendance. Jock, of course, the host for the evening, was there, as well as Spencer Thorneycroft. Doctor Martin Kemp, one of five general practitioners in the town and a recent arrival from Johannesburg was attending for the first time. Don Gammon, a partner in the Gammon Brothers business which owned several Atlantic filling stations as well as the Dodge franchise for Manicaland, rounded out the school.

It was during the third game, a well-played affair by Don Gammon who had managed to keep everyone's money in the game with some very canny bidding, that the subject of Blackie Schwartz' recent arrest came up in the conversation. His arrest had been emblazoned on the front page of the Umtali Post the previous Tuesday. Of even greater interest to the easily scandalised white community was the fact that, alongside the news article, a photograph had been published which showed the mine manager chained to his fellow, black, thieves.

"I wonder what Eddie Evans will do now?" asked Gammon, "he's short a mine manager, and a pretty good one from what I heard."

"If good means dishonest, then I suppose you're right." harrumphed Jock Mitchell, stealthily fanning his cards.

"Well, I didn't mean to imply that I condone what he did, but I think even Eddie would agree that the Revue ran damned efficiently. And anyway, Jock, whatever happened to the presumption of innocence?"

"Do you think Eddie would be open to hiring a new manager?" asked Jock after a few moments of silence, thinking of his wife's younger brother who had recently joined them from Scotland.

Iain Murdoch had been in two wars and wounded in both. During the Anglo-Boer War he had been at Magersfontein with the Blackwatch and had witnessed his general, Andy Wauchope, fall under a hail of Boer bullets on December 11th, 1899. Murdoch had been a newly-commissioned subaltern, full of jingo zeal for the British cause, but lying under a scorching tropic sun with no water and only a kilt to protect his lily-white legs soon wilted his bravado. Later in the day, when the young Scot thought it couldn't get any worse, a Boer sniper had shot him through the upper arm, shattering his humerus in two places.

Fifteen years later, at the outbreak of the Great War, his arm still weaker than it should have been, Iain had volunteered to serve with his old regiment as a territorial soldier. By then thirty-five years old, he was one of the most experienced of his company when it went into action in Flanders. By the end of the first day, he was the most senior man still alive and unwounded and was given a field promotion to brevet captain. Then, at the end of 1916, he had been badly wounded by shrapnel during heavy shelling of British positions near Ypres. His physical wounds gradually healed, but the mental wounds were less obvious, and, if anything, far more serious.

Jock's wife Elsie had invited the wounded warrior to come out and stay with her and her husband in sunny Rhodesia where the weather, she thought, would be more conducive to healing than the grey weather of the Scottish Highlands.

Between the two wars, through his regimental connections, Iain had obtained employment at a coal mine near Nidrie and over time had been promoted to Assistant Mine Manager. Elsie thought that a management position on a Rhodesian mine might be something he could look at. Thus, when she read the Schwartz story in the newspaper, she had mentioned to Jock that 'we must talk to Eddie Evans, see if he might need a new mine manager'.

"Good white men are very difficult to find at the moment," said Don Gammon, carefully eyeing his hand. "We've been trying to get a parts manager for ages now. Nothing doing. All the good'uns are still away in Europe. And if they didn't volunteer, I don't want 'em. No 'white feather' men for me. Oh no sir, not for me."

"Elsie has a brother who is with us at the moment," said Jock. "Wounded in action at Ypres, he was. He's mending slowly, but I think he'd mend faster if he had a decent job to go to each day."

"Bella Evans is a patient of mine," said Martin Kemp. "When next I see her I'll mention your brother-in-law to her, you never know. What's his name, Jock?"

"Murdoch's his name, Iain Murdoch. Thanks, Marty, very kind of you."

§

True to his word and after he had finished examining a very pregnant Bella Evans, Martin Kemp raised the subject of the visiting war-hero, Iain Murdoch. Bella made no promises, but agreed to ask her husband whether he may have a position for a wounded soldier.

§

The following day, armed with directions provided by Jock Mitchell, Iain Murdoch drove out to the Rezende Mine in his brother-in-law's Model T Runabout for a ten o'clock meeting with the owner, Eddie Evans. He brought with him a biscuit tin decorated with an artist's impression of Edinburgh Rock. Contained within it were two dozen of Elsie Mitchell's prize-winning short-bread cookies.

Eddie was impressed with the man's knowledge of mining, albeit in a coal setting rather than hard-rock, but he felt the man could easily learn the nuances of gold-mining. As a staunch Presbyterian, it was unlikely that the demon booze would be a problem for the newly-arrived Scotsman either. Eddie would have preferred that Murdoch be a married man, but Rhodesia had never had a surfeit of single unmarried ladies and so there were many men in the country who had waited to marry until well into their forties.

They quickly agreed on start dates (the next day), pay scales (half of what Blackie Schwartz had been earning, plus a production bonus). Fifty-eight minutes after the interview had begun with a cup of tea and a short-bread cookie, Iain Murdoch became just the second manager of the Revue Mine.

At precisely eleven o'clock, as the new manager stood outside Eddie's office opening the Model T's front door, and with Samuel looking on from the doorway of his office, the planned morning blast took place deep within the mine. To everyone else who worked on the mine-site it was not at all unusual, just a deep-throated roar accompanied by a cloud of brown dust billowing out of the portal. To Iain Murdoch, however, not long removed from the killing fields of France and Flanders, it was something else entirely. He threw himself flat upon the dirt ground behind the motor-car, his hands covering his head, and lay there for several minutes, quivering.

Eddie and Samuel both ran down the verandah steps to assist the new man, thinking that perhaps he may have experienced some medical event, a stroke or a heart attack. They lifted him to his legs but, shaking them off short-temperedly, he proceeded to climb into the car as though absolutely nothing had happened.

Afterwards, Eddie wondered if he had made the right decision in hiring Elsie Mitchell's brother.

"Any plans for tomorrow, Samuel?" asked Eddie. "I think we should both go to Revue and ease the new man into his position."

"Nothing tomorrow, boss, but right now I'd like to head back to the mission, if you don't mind."

Just then the phone rang in Eddie's office. He held his hand up, silently signalling Samuel not to go.

"What's that, Spencer? The line's bad. Say again. Yes, yes, right, I'll tell him." And Eddie hung up the phone on its Y-shaped harness.

"Samuel, that was Spencer Thorneycroft on the line from Umtali. They've found another body at the mission. He says it could well be natural causes but wants you to investigate as soon as possible. Just to be sure, you know."

"Did he say who it was?"

"Someone by the name of Hove." Eddie glanced down at the note he had written during the phone call. "Lucas Hove. An elderly man. He worked at the mission as a night-watchman."

Chapter 16

Samuel ran for his motor-cycle and, forsaking the unreliable and tiring kick-start method, did a running start, and then, once he had built up a good momentum, jumped on sideways and simultaneously let out the clutch. The Royal Enfield didn't let him down and he sped out of the mine-site in a cloud of dust.

Not a mile up the road he came across Iain Murdoch puttering along in his brother-in-law's Model T blowing up a storm of dust behind him, despite his low speed.

After eating his dust for a couple of minutes, Samuel opened up the throttle and blew by the Scotsman as though he were standing still.

When he arrived at the mission, Samuel went straight up to the school administration block. The noise of the motor-cycle brought Mr. Sykes outside, his face looking grim.

"I suppose you've heard, Mr. Kumalo? Superintendent Thorneycroft said he would ask you to come out and do the initial investigation."

"Yes, I received his message. It said that Lucas had been found deceased. Is that correct?"

"Yes, quite so. His grand-daughter became concerned when he never came back for his breakfast, or perhaps I should say dinner, this morning. His shift ends at six o'clock, and at seven she started making enquiries of her neighbours and so on. They then started a search of his normal beat and that's when he was found, almost in the same place where Gideon's body was found."

"Near that kopje with the iron-wood tree growing alongside the giant rock?"

"Exactly. What do you think this is all about, Kumalo? I'm very concerned that accounts of these deaths not get back to my headquarters in Dallas. It doesn't speak well of the mission in general and of this school in particular."

"I think you may be over-reacting, Mr. Sykes. For all we know this could have been a natural event. Lucas was quite old and not in very good health, you know."

"Yes, yes, but it seems such a coincidence that he was found at the same place where Gideon was found."

"Now that *is* a little strange, I must agree. But let us not jump to conclusions until I have completed my investigation. Now, let me get to the body."

Lucas lay face down on the dried leaves under the iron-wood tree. There did not appear to be any wounds, even after Samuel had carefully removed the old man's black great-coat and inspected his clothes for any signs of blood. Nothing that he could see. To all intents and purposes, the old man had collapsed some time during the night and died on the spot.

Samuel felt under Lucas' armpit. It was not warm, but certainly not cold, and rigor-mortis had only just recently begun. Samuel thought that the man had not been dead for more than five hours, putting his death at somewhere around six this morning, just at the time he would have been heading home to Charity and a nice hot meal. Doc Snelgar would be able to render a more precise verdict on time of death once he received the body.

§

Upon hearing Samuel's opinion that the old man had probably died of natural causes, Mr. Sykes arranged to have a hearse come out to take Lucas' body to a funeral chapel in Umtali. Samuel had a word with the driver when he arrived, and the two agreed that his destination would be altered to Umtali General Hospital in care of Doctor Snelgar. Always pays to cover one's backside thought Samuel.

§

"Charity!" he shouted. *"Sisi!"*

172

Samuel stood outside Lucas' small cottage, calling for the old man's grand-daughter.

Finally she appeared from the gloom of the thatched building, her eyes red from crying and looking very, very sad.

"I am so sorry for your great loss, Charity. Your grandfather was a good man."

She nodded and blew her nose loudly on an apron she wore around her waist.

"Was he perhaps feeling ill? Did he say anything to you before he headed out last night?"

"No, he was fine. He had a big meal at five and headed off as usual at six. There seemed to be nothing wrong with him. He did say he wanted to check out that place where Gideon was found. He said he had seen some lights and heard some noises there very early yesterday morning."

Interesting, thought Samuel. Very interesting.

"Charity, what will you do now that your grandfather is deceased?"

"I will return to my *babamukuru's* house in Umtali. School starts again in two weeks."

Samuel made his way back to the school complex. He needed to see Mr. Sykes. The headmaster's office door was closed. Samuel could hear muffled voices coming from within. He was in the process of placing his ear against the door when it was violently thrust open and out flew a female figure, so quickly that he was almost bowled over. It was Isobel Takwanda, the young bespectacled teacher, and she was sobbing.

Samuel tapped lightly on the door then entered unbidden. Mr. Sykes sat at his desk, his head buried in his hands.

"Is there something troubling you Mr. Sykes?" he asked.

Sykes' head flew out of the cradle formed by his hands and Samuel could see that he, too, had been weeping. Was it sorrow for the old man who had died? I doubt it, thought Samuel, I doubt it very much.

"Mr. Sykes, I must apologise for troubling you, but I have some more questions for you"

"Oh, surely not now, not at a time like this? Can't you see that we are all under terrible emotional stress right now? Everything seems to be going wrong of a sudden. Please!"

"Unfortunately, Mr. Sykes, time waits for no man, and I have an investigation to complete."

"Well, I guess I'll have to help you, I don't want to seem un-Christian. What is it, then?"

"Some weeks ago, you signed a purchase order for 50 milligrams of potassium cyanide from Mitchell's Pharmacy. Was it perhaps for scientific experiments in the chemistry classes here at the mission school?"

"Good God, no, of course not! This is just an elementary school, we don't offer chemistry courses here. That subject is only tackled by high school students."

"That is exactly what I thought, sir. But nevertheless, you *did* order the chemical. Your signature is on the purchase order."

"That could well be, Kumalo. You see I am not only the headmaster of the school; I also oversee finances, purchases, administration, and so on for the entire Mission. So yes, I would almost certainly have signed the purchase order, just as I sign every other purchase order."

"But the originator of the order, let's say someone at the hospital, for example, must have certified that the product was needed? Not so?"

"Yes, that's exactly how it works. Hold on a minute," and, sighing impatiently, Sykes got up and went over to a metal filing cabinet marked 'Accounts'. Opening the drawer, he flipped through several files before coming back with one and sitting down behind his desk again.

"Here we are," he said finally, "50 milligrams of Potassium Cyanide ordered on January 5th, received into stores on January 11th."

"Good. But who made the requisition, sir?"

"Sister Mukarakate"

§

The plump nursing sister was seated in a chair at the front reception desk when Samuel dismounted from his motor-cycle and climbed the five stairs to the mission hospital entrance.

"Mister Kumalo! How nice to see you again," she gushed, a big smile on her round face. She had a pen in one hand and was writing in a register. "I won't be a minute, just need to finish this patient report." She returned to her task.

Finishing the report with a flourish of her pen, the good sister came around to the front of the reception desk.

"Now, my good sir, what can I do for you today? Oh, but first I should really ask, how is your back?"

"It is quite well, thank you. I no longer have any more pain, so I suppose you could say I am now healed. There are two things I am here for, Sister; the first concerns old Lucas, the school night-watchman."

Before he could ask his question, Sister Mukarakate lowered her eyes and said, "What a shock to all of us. He was such a good man, you know, raising his son's daughter as if she were his own. But I suppose none of us knows when his time is up on heaven's clock."

"Yes, I know what you mean, sister. Was he a frequent patient at the hospital here? Did he have any ailments that might have been life-threatening?"

"He suffered very badly from rheumatoid arthritis, especially in his fingers and toes. As a result, he found it quite difficult to walk. But apart from that, no, I should have thought he was in fairly good condition. We gave him aspirin for the pain, that is all."

Samuel was busy taking notes. "Nothing else?"

"No, not from the hospital. However, being an older man, of the old school, shall we say, he may still have trusted in the medicinal powers of an *ng'anga*, a traditional healer. In fact I'm sure he said something about getting *mushonga* from an *ng'anga* who lives in a small hut over there," and she pointed north, 'on the road to Penhalonga."

Interesting. Medicine from a traditional healer? That fact definitely warranted more investigation.

"One more thing, sister. A few weeks ago you signed a requisition for 50 mg of potassium cyanide. What do you use that particular chemical for in the hospital? And do you have any left?"

"Oh, those poisonous crystals? In the small bottle? We don't use that in the hospital. I ordered it for Doctor Jefferson. He has been collecting African insects, butterflies and so on, ever since he arrived in this country. And before that in America. He is, how do you say, an entomologist. Also a lepidopterist, he collects butterflies. An amateur. It is his hobby. He uses the gas from those crystals to kill the insects. He says they die very quickly and without any damage to their delicate wings etc. Then he can mount them for display. He says his collection of African butterflies is almost as good as the one in the Cape Town museum."

"Thank you, sister, you have been most helpful. I'll let you get on with your patient reports."

Samuel wasn't sure what he should do next. He wanted to visit Doc Snelgar who by now should have examined old Lucas' body. But he also wanted to visit the *ng'anga*, find out what other traditional medicine, *mushonga*, Lucas might have been ingesting. Problem was, he wasn't really sure where the *ng'anga's* hut was located, and to find it might involve a bit of a search. It can wait, he thought, and headed off for Umtali and the evil-smelling bowels of the general hospital.

§

"For a man of his age," opined the grizzled doctor, standing alongside Lucas' body, "he was in remarkably good condition. Bad arthritis, but it wasn't life-threatening. I would imagine he didn't walk very fast. These calcified growths here and here," and he pointed with a wooden ruler to large bulges near Lucas' big toes and heels, "would have restricted his mobility."

"So you're saying he died of natural causes?"

"Did I say that, Samuel, or are you just putting words in my mouth? I can tell you for sure that his heart stopped beating, so that is natural, yes, but *why* did it stop beating, now *that* is the important question."

"Oh, come on, doc, don't keep me in suspense."

"I will be saying on my official examiner's report that his heart showed strong evidence of tachycardia and atrial fibrillation which, I believe, combined to cause a massive stroke. He exhibits many of the risk factors that are associated with tachycardia. For example, I presume from

178

my overall observation that he is over sixty years of age, that's one risk factor. From the look of his teeth and lungs he would appear to be a heavy smoker, so there's another. I haven't had the blood tests back from the lab yet, but I suspect that we may find some kind of stimulant. Maybe, maybe not."

"Stimulant? Like what, for example?"

"Have you ever heard of a drug called cocaine? It's used in many medicinal preparations, especially over the counter products for stomach ailments etc. Even in a popular soft drink called Coca-Cola. Some people use the pure form as a stimulant, but too much of it would cause the heart to do the same thing that Lucas' heart did. With similar outcomes. Fortunately, cocaine is not that easy to get hold of in this country. And, of course, this is all just sheer speculation on my part. I won't know anything until I get the blood tests back from the lab."

Just then there was a knock on Doc Snelgar's door and in walked a young lady whom Samuel had not met before. She had dark hair, almost black, lush and thick, with natural curls fighting against the strictures of a blue laboratory cap. She handed Snelgar a sheet with a number of ciphers written on it, and then turned to leave, glancing at the tall Matabele standing there.

"Thanks very much, Helen, appreciate the quick turn-around. Oh, sorry, how ill-mannered of me. Helen, this is Samuel Kumalo, Samuel, meet Helen Cave. Samuel used to work for BSAP Umtali until he went off to fight in France."

"And Tanganyika." said Samuel.

"Yes, of course, Tanganyika, too. Just returned and decided to go back to civilian life. He works for Eddie Evans now, out at the Rezende Mine in Penhalonga. You must have met Bella Evans?"

"Yes, of course," replied Helen, smiling pleasantly, "she's one of the leading lights in the Umtali Women's Institute."

After Helen had gone, leaving in her wake a delicate aroma of eau de cologne, Samuel said, "Well, doc?"

The doctor seemed to be day-dreaming, completely in a world of his own. Samuel wondered if it had anything to do with the very obvious allure of a certain Helen Cave. This Doc Snelgar was turning out to be quite the Lothario if it was true. First it had been Connie Snyman and now Helen Cave.

Snelgar snapped out of his reverie and looked down at the numbers Helen had put into his hand.

"Oh," he said, his eyebrows arching with surprise. "That's funny. It seems that our good man here got on the wrong end of a deadly dose of atropine."

"What's that?' asked Samuel, ready with his pad and a pencil.

"It's the active chemical in Belladonna, or deadly nightshade. It's a plant. It's sometimes used to alleviate the symptoms of rheumatism, so he may have taken it for that reason. Unfortunately, he must have taken too much and it killed him."

"Do you think it might be something he could have obtained from an *ng'anga*?" He thought the name rather strange. Eddie's wife's name was Bella. Years ago he had asked her what the name meant and she had told him it meant pretty or even beautiful in the Italian language. He wondered what belladonna could mean. He made a mental note to ask Mrs. Pennefather when next he saw her. She seemed to know everything about plants.

"Yes, it could be, those *ng'angas* are a clever bunch. But the plant is not indigenous to southern Africa, you know, and generally the *ng'angas* obtain their herbs from local sources. I would say that you need to keep prying. At least you know what did him in. But whether it was accidently by his own hand or not will have to await completion of my formal autopsy. Until we know for sure, I will have to give an indeterminate, open ruling in my report."

"Doc, one last thing," said Samuel, halfway to the door. He turned and came back to the long sink.

"Didn't you get your medical degree at Edinburgh University?"

"Yes, I did, more years ago than I care to remember."

"The mission doctor got his OBGYN designation at Edinburgh medical school. Do you think you'd be able to make some enquiries of your old school. Just to confirm that he does indeed have the OBGYN designation. It's just a little loose string I need to tidy up."

"Well, Samuel, funny you should ask. The registrar of the college of medicine is an old school chum of mine – Hugh Stewart is his name. I'll send him a cable. I think he'll get a kick out of hearing from his old schoolmate after all these years!"

Chapter 17

Sister Mukarakate's directions to the *ng'anga's* kraal had been extremely vague, and after half an hour of slow riding, Samuel still had not found anything that remotely resembled the nurse's description of the traditional healer's abode. Finally, looking at his watch and seeing how late it had become, he opened up the throttle and headed on towards Penhalonga, Agnes, Hastings and Farai.

Farai! Samuel had a brain flash. If anyone knew where the *ng'anga* lived, it would be Farai. These herd boys seemed to know everything that went on in the community.

Farai and Hastings were playing in the gravel roadway outside the house. Farai had fabricated a motor car from small pieces of wire, with a long bamboo rod which he used to push and steer it with. Hastings was beaming with happiness at this remarkable toy, and as Samuel parked the Royal Enfield, he called out "See, *baba*, see my car. Farai made it for me!"

"Farai, you did a good job. It looks very realistic. Come boys, let's go inside now. *Amai* will be ready for supper very soon." Samuel picked up his son, and they all went inside to join Agnes who was almost ready to serve the evening meal.

As they ate, Samuel looked at Farai. In the short time that he had been living with them, he had filled out very nicely; his skin had a glow to it that had not been in evidence before. His eyes, too, had a life to them, a glint which hinted at intelligence beyond that which books could provide.

"Farai?"

"*Baba?*"

"Sister Mukarakate told me that there is a certain *ng'anga* who lives in seclusion in a hut near the road between here and Old Umtali mission. Do you know this man?"

"Everyone knows this man. Everyone fears this man."

"But where does he live? And why do people fear him?"

"His hut is very close to the road but you cannot see it from the road. It is in a small valley among some Msasa trees. And it is not far from the mission driveway. No more than a ten or fifteen minute walk. Perhaps I can show you tomorrow?"

"And what about school? No, my son, I will find it myself."

"But *baba*, you may not be successful."

"No arguments, Farai," said Agnes. "You must go to school tomorrow. Now eat your food! But first, tell me, why do people fear him?"

"People say that he knows all about poisons, how to make them from plants and seeds, and for the right price he will sell you these poisons. Oh yes, he is a man to be feared, for sure."

§

After meeting with Eddie early the following morning, and agreeing that they would both head off to Revue upon his return from the *ng'anga*, Samuel fired up the Royal Enfield and headed off towards the mission. Much to his chagrin, he had no more success in finding the *ng'anga's* hut than he had had the previous afternoon, and eventually, with a certain amount of disgust, turned the bike around and headed back to Penhalonga.

§

Bella was in the midst of a spelling bee when Samuel knocked on the school-room door and walked in. "Sorry, Miss Bella," he said, "I need Farai for a little while."

From the thunderous look on his face, Bella realised it would be entirely futile to object.

"Not a word, Farai. Just get on the motor-cycle."

"So? You couldn't find...."

"I said, not a word!" Samuel's anger masked a great deal of embarrassment.

§

At Farai's instruction, Samuel parked the Royal Enfield in the shade of a fruit-filled *mahobohobo* tree and the two of them set off on foot, Farai leading the way, happily chewing on one of the small round berries he had plucked from the tree. No more than three minutes later they found themselves in the clean-swept yard of a pole and mud hut. Its roof was made of grass, but not neatly thatched like other traditional dwellings. This one looked bedraggled, as though birds had been allowed to pull grass from the thatch to make their nests in the Msasa trees that surrounded the hut.

Samuel could see smoke coming through the apex of the conical thatch roof and heaved a sigh of relief that this trip and Farai's absence from school had not been in vain.

Samuel approached the solitary hut with some trepidation, for *ng'angas* are considered to have great powers amongst the tribes of Africa. The door was made with several hand-hewn planks of wood laced together with baling wire. More wire looped several times at top and bottom of the doorpost acted as hinges. Whoever lived here was not one who bothered much with luxury, thought Samuel.

He knocked on the door, two raps, and a high-pitched voice bade him enter. As sunlight flooded the hut, he could see a wizened, wrinkled bundle sitting on the far side of a small fire, blue smoke curling listlessly towards the thatched roof. The *ng'anga's* sex was indeterminate, could easily have been a woman. The bundle was dressed in animal skins; they looked to be monkey, and was seated on a kaross made of rock-rabbit skins. It probably also serves as his blanket at night, thought Samuel.

186

"So you are the Matabele prince, grandson of the great elephant?" the *ng'anga* began in his high-pitched voice, and threw some material into the fire which caused it to hiss and crackle and give off sparks. "Sit down, Samuel Kumalo."

Samuel squatted on his haunches. How does this person know so much about me? he wondered.

The *ng'anga* took out a leather pouch and began filling a brown stained wooden pipe with some of the pouch's contents, then leaned forward and took an ember from the fire. An aromatic, cloying smell soon filled the hut as he puffed on the thin stem of the pipe. *Mbanje*, thought Samuel. He's smoking marijuana! No wonder his eyes are so red. In his early days with the police Samuel had been part of a marijuana eradication team. He knew the smell well.

"*Baba*," he began, respectfully. "I have come to ask you some questions regarding the night-watchman at the mission school."

"He is dead."

"Yes, *baba*, how did you know, did someone tell you?"

"No-one comes here to socialize; they only come for my medicine. No-one told me. I knew it. The crows talk to me from the Msasa trees."

Just then there came a sound of crows cawing in the trees high above the hut and despite the fire in front of him a

187

chill feeling went up and down Samuel's spine and the hairs on the back of his neck stood up.

"When we examined his body at the hospital we found some medicine which we think caused his death. It is made from flowers. Did you give it to him? He may have taken too much, and that is what caused his death."

"That man *did* come to me, but not for medicine, although my potions could have helped him with his swollen fingers and toes. No, he came to me to try to help him with his grand-daughter. He wanted to know who had made her pregnant. She is very young and he was very angry at whoever had done this thing. He needed to know."

"And? Did you tell him who the father was?"

"No. I gave him a tool to divine the name."

"A tool? What tool?"

"It was a warthog's tusk."

Samuel sat there on his haunches, speechless at this astounding information. It raised so many other questions, and he realised that he was again no closer to a solution to Gideon's murder now than he had been on the day of his wedding when he had first noticed the sad old lady. And now a potential, nay, a very strong suspect given what the *ng'anga* had just told him, was also dead. And the death of old Lucas seemed to be quite as suspicious as that of Gideon. But if the night-watchman *had* killed Gideon and Samuel doubted that such an old, infirm man had the strength to overcome a young man of twenty-five, then who had killed Lucas? But in all of this, the over-riding issue was *why*? Yes, he could see Lucas having the motive – after all Gideon had sired an out-of-wedlock child with an under-age student, his grand-daughter, and certainly *that* could be motive enough. But as Samuel understood it, Charity had lost the child, so presumably Lucas' motive should have evaporated somewhat.

"*Baba*," said Samuel, for there was something bothering him. "What did that warthog's tusk look like?"

The old man leaned over and took hold of a leather bag. It rattled as he lifted it towards him. He reached inside and pulled out a tusk.

"It was the mate to this one," said the *ng'anga*, and held up a large tusk, which curved almost into a circle.

Finally, his legs almost numb from their enforced lack of circulation, Samuel rose unsteadily from his haunches. He made his thanks to the aged *ng'anga*, passing over two silver half-crowns that tinkled as they fell into the *ng'anga's* gnarled hand.

Samuel stood outside in the sun for a few minutes gathering his thoughts. Finally, he thought, I think I have the answer to this riddle of the warthog's tusk. But another side of him was torn between the mission murders and his duties at the two Evans' mines. Then Farai came sloping silently out from the glade of Msasa trees and seeing him spurred Samuel to a decision.

"Come on Farai, you've had too much time away from school. Let's go, my boy."

§

"Samuel! I'm so glad to see you've made a complete recovery. And who is this young man you have with you?"

"My name is Farai and I am the new son of Samuel and Agnes Kumalo," said Farai proudly, his chest puffed out, a big broad grin on his face.

Mrs. Pennefather smiled at the young boy perched on the back of the Royal Enfield. "I am very pleased to meet you, Farai. And I am Mrs. Pennefather. I bet you would like a mango. Yes?"

Samuel had been rather hoping that a quick detour to the Pennefather oasis might result in some more fruit. Agnes had been exceedingly pleased with the tray he had brought back with him the last time he had visited Mrs. Pennefather.

"Mrs. P," he said, "Agnes was wondering if we could buy some more fruit from you. That last tray was so very good and sweet-tasting."

"Buy? I wouldn't hear of it. You come with me and we'll pick some fresh fruit off the trees." And with that she strode away in a very businesslike way, picking up a wicker basket from the back verandah as she passed.

Farai was sent up into a large avocado tree to pick the fruit and while he was climbing, Samuel asked the old lady about some of the plants that grew there in such profusion.

"Have you ever heard of a plant called Bella-something?" he asked.

"Bella-something? Do you mean Belladonna?"

"Yes, you are exactly right. That is the name, Belladonna. What is it, Mrs. P?"

"Come, I'll show you, I actually have a couple of shrubs in my garden." She moved him off to another area of the garden.

"Here it is, Samuel. It's not indigenous to Rhodesia, you know, but it does rather well, as you can see." She gestured towards a shrub with strange looking rubbery leaves and black berries. "You know that it's quite poisonous, don't you? In England it's called Deadly Nightshade. Hmmm, that's funny."

"What's funny?"

"There seems to have been some pruning going on here. I didn't do it. I wonder if Langson took it upon himself to do it without telling me. That's naughty if he did, because this is not the right time of year to prune this shrub." She paused, deep in thought, and then called out "Lang-son!" at the top of her voice. Samuel couldn't believe that a woman of such slight build and great age could have a voice as powerful as Mrs. Pennefather's.

From the far end of the garden came a plaintive, "Madam?" and a minute or so later a middle-aged gardener appeared, breathless from running at the sound of his lady's call.

191

"Langson, did you do this?" Mrs. Pennefather pulled one of the Belladonna's clipped branches towards her. "This pruning?"

"No madam, it was not I. We should ask Philemon, he may know."

Langson ran off to find his assistant who was apparently dealing with compost-making at a far end of the property. Five minutes later the two of them were back.

"Philemon, did you cut this bush? Don't worry, I am not angry, I just need to know the truth."

"Yes, Madam, it was I. But I did it for a white boss when you were away in Umtali. He came here looking for some examples of English plants. I thought it would be alright. Sorry, madam."

"No, no, don't worry about it, Philemon. Who was this white man? Do I know him? Is he from around here, or visiting from away?"

"He is the big boss from the Old Umtali mission."

"Mr. Sykes?" Samuel interjected.

"Yes, that is the very one."

A look of recollection came over Mrs. Pennefather's face.

"Ah yes, Mr. Sykes," she said, "the American gentleman. That's right. He was here at my spring garden party last year. I hold one every year. He told me there was someone at the mission who was an avid collector of rare and unusual flora. I told him about the Belladonna, but I told him about many other rare plants that I have here, too. My collection of Gloriosa, you know, Flame Lilies, for example, is the best in Rhodesia. The curator of Rondebosch Gardens in Cape Town has even come to see them. And you know, Samuel, Gloriosa is also a dangerous, very poisonous plant."

And now Samuel had even more to think about. This case was getting ever more convoluted. Sykes? A potential suspect? Why on earth would Sykes want to murder the old night-watchman? It just didn't make sense.

Nothing made any sense.

Chapter 18

The Revue mine was a flurry of activity as Eddie and Samuel pulled in through the big wire-laced gates. There was a security guard on duty who signed them in. He came from inside a small sentry-house and looked smart and soldierly. This is all new, thought Eddie. My new man is obviously making changes.

They parked the Model T outside the manager's office and climbed the four or five stairs up onto the verandah that shielded the office block from the fiercest sun. The door marked MINE MANAGER was closed and locked, so Eddie and Samuel walked down to the mill room and its adjacent laboratory. The mill was banging away, and again, Eddie could find no fault with the way everything was running. In fact, he was quite impressed. For a fellow who had no gold-mining experience, Jock Mitchell's brother-in-law seemed to be doing a fine job.

They walked out of the dark mill-room squinting against the bright afternoon sun and that's when they both heard Murdoch screaming. Not shouting, which in certain circumstances could be considered as a seldom-used management tool, but rather wild, banshee screaming, which, in Eddie's view, should never be used by a manager on his subordinates under any circumstances.

Murdoch was standing at the mine portal, his eyes bulging with anger, his mouth and chin speckled with spit. His attention and ire seemed to be focused on Jeremiah, the shift-boss. Eddie looked at his watch. Three o'clock and this must be the morning shift coming off after their eight-hour day. Murdoch seemed apoplectic, his hand, holding a clip-board, visibly shaking with rage.

"Afternoon, Murdoch," said Eddie, "what's going on here, then?"

"These black bastards have been doing nothing today! Lazy fucking bastards! Look here and he thrust his clipboard towards Eddie, who ignored it. "They've done seventeen coco-pans today. Seventeen! Their quota is forty-two. I've a good mind to dock them their wages!"

"But boss," stuttered Jeremiah.

"Don't bloody *but* me, you lazy good-for-nothing scoundrel. How you came to be a shift-boss is beyond me. If I had my way, you'd be in the boiler room as a stoker."

"Jeremiah," said Eddie, very calmly, "tell me what happened on your shift today." Turning to Murdoch he said, very calmly and evenly, "Iain, please don't interrupt."

"Everything was going very well, Boss Eddie. It's all in my report, but he won't read it."

"Jeremiah, just tell me what happened."

"A few minutes after our eleven o'clock tea break, we heard a big noise in number two entry and big clouds of dust came boiling out. We knew it had to be a bad roof-fall, and not five minutes before we had all been in that very place. The roof-fall was at least fourteen feet deep, so we spent most of the balance of the shift mucking out the entry and re-setting timbers. We're lucky we never lost anyone."

"Thank-you, Jeremiah. Now go and have a shower and change, and I'll see you at the shifter's office at four o'clock." Eddie turned to Murdoch. "We need to talk, Iain. Come with me."

Samuel excused himself. He had a feeling that Murdoch was about to receive a good bollocking. Eddie and Murdoch went into the latter's office.

Eddie rounded on his new manager.

"If I *ever* hear you speaking to the men in that tone of voice again, Murdoch, you will wish that you had never left Scotland." Eddie was speaking in a voice that was scarcely above a whisper, but there was no mistaking his intent.

"Evans Consolidated treats its people, *all of them*, top to bottom, with respect, d'you understand? Respect. That's all I ask. That man Jeremiah has forgotten more about mining than you will ever know. Use him as a resource, as an equal rather than an underling, and you will find how much more you will get out of everybody. Frankly, I am very disappointed in you, Murdoch. If this ever happens again I'll have to let you go. Understood?"

"Yes, sir, Mr. Evans. Understood. But you do realise that I was just trying to do my best by the company?"

"If that was your best then we have a problem. These men are not a platoon of soldiers on the Western Front. They are putting their lives in danger every minute of every shift they spend underground. Remember that."

§

On the road back to Rezende, Samuel brought Eddie up to date on the Gideon murder case.

"I apologise for not having been around much, *Inkosi*, but this Gideon case is taking me in directions that I never thought possible."

"Any suspects?"

"At first there were none, but now there are too many. And to confuse the case even more, the man who found Gideon's body has died. We're not yet sure how, but I believe he, too, may have been murdered. That was the message you received from Superintendent Thorneycroft"

"That's not what Snelgar told me at the golf club last evening. He said he was giving an open or indeterminate verdict on the Lucas Hove case."

"Legally speaking that may be so, but I am treating it as a murder. I have found out some things today which lead me to suspect that his death was deliberate. And I suspect that whoever killed the old man also killed Gideon, but I just don't know how and, most frustrating of all, why."

"Look, Samuel, you must take all the time you need to get the two cases solved. This is a community thing and, what is more, Gideon's mother lives on the Rezende, so there's the company connection as well."

§

Later on, after the evening meal, Samuel sat with Hastings and Farai. Hastings was busy with a 120-piece jigsaw puzzle and Samuel was amazed at how quickly the three-year-old was able to recognize the pieces and fit them into their appropriate slots. Farai, for his part, seemed to be making good progress with his lessons, although Samuel suspected that he would far prefer to be out on the motorcycle with him or climbing an avocado-pear tree.

Finally, with the two boys having gone to their beds, Samuel took out his Gideon file and brought it up to date. As he scratched away, he allowed his mind to flow freely. There seems to be a story, he thought, a highly-convoluted story of a number of people at the Old Umtali mission; a story of love, lost love, pregnancy, lost pregnancy, a good man whom everybody liked now dead, his death made to look like a vicious animal attack. And then the death of a harmless old man, or was he so harmless? By the time he had finished writing up his notes, he was tired, ready for bed, his eyes sore and fingers cramped from writing in his meticulous script; but he believed he might just have a scenario as to what had happened at the Old Umtali mission.

But scenarios and the truth do not always coincide.

Chapter 19

That feeling of being torn between two competing duties had been effectively removed by the conversation he had had with Eddie Evans. Samuel felt he could now devote all his energies to the Gideon murder, and to the Lucas death, which, despite Doc Snelgar's reservations, he now firmly believed to be a murder.

His 'to do' list that day as he bade Agnes and Hastings goodbye was a short one, but he knew that, as always seemed to happen, one thing would lead to another. It would probably be many hours before he would be back with his family again.

Farai jumped aboard the Royal Enfield for the short trip to Bella's village school. Outside the small, corrugated-iron-roofed building he jumped off the motor-cycle and hugged Samuel goodbye. All the young lad's emotional reticence seemed to have been blown away by the solid feeling of family and good food, both of which had been in extremely limited supply in his short life.

Now, alone on the bike, Samuel was able to go over the items on his list.

Number one: Talk to Sykes; find out who was the avid collector of rare flora for whom he had obtained the Belladonna clippings.

Number two: Charity; what could she tell him about the warthog's tusk? Did she know her grandfather had been given one by the *ng'anga* to root out the father of her unborn child?

Number three: what was the connection between Sykes and Isobel Takwanda? Why had she left his office so upset?

Number four: Barry Simcoe; he needed to be brought up to date on recent developments.

Number five: Doc Snelgar; confirm that he was still open-minded on Lucas' death. There didn't seem much point in investigating a natural cause death if that was what it was.

Number six: Jock Mitchell; see what he could tell Samuel about poison-making using noxious plants.

§

Mr. Sykes was in his office and 'wouldn't be a second' as he finished off some paperwork. He was as good as his word and a minute or so later, he ushered Samuel into his office.

"Y'all care for a cup of coffee, Mistuh Kumalo?" he asked Samuel who continued to struggle a little understanding the man's strong western Tennessee accent.

"Thank you, sir, coffee would be nice."

They talked in that desultory way non-strangers do while they waited for the coffee to arrive, brought in by a pleasant young lady, who smiled and curtsied politely. Samuel realised she was a young lady of traditional values and as she laid down the tray he said, *"Otenda makwende,"* and clapped his hands softly in thanks. She smiled sweetly, her eyes demurely turned down, then left as quietly as she had arrived.

"You speak Chishona pretty well for a Matabele, Mistuh Kumalo. Sorry to digress, sir, what was it you wanted to see me about?"

"Well," began Samuel, unsure how to approach his question. "Mrs. Pennefather's gardener tells me that you recently took plant cuttings from her garden."

"Well, I didn't just take them. I asked for them, and her gardener gave them to me. I hope they are not saying I stole them? I certainly hope not. I had been at a garden party put on by Mrs. Pennefather late last year and she had basically given me an open invitation to come and take samples for our own botanical garden here at the mission. The day I went there, she had gone away to Umtali, if I remember rightly, but I was sure she wouldn't mind."

"Oh no, not at all, in fact I think she is quite proud that you deemed her plants to be of sufficient interest to warrant planting them in the mission garden. Do you like gardening Mr. Sykes?"

"Goodness, no, not me. I don't have a green thumb. If I plant something you can be guaranteed it will have wilted and died within a few days! Oh no, the mission garden is the brainchild of our good Doctor Jefferson. We were talking about my visit to Mrs. Pennefather's garden, and he asked me if I could possibly get certain plants for our garden. They were mainly exotic specimens, plants that are not indigenous to this country."

Samuel was nodding his head, at the same time scratching brief notes with his pencil in his spiral-bound notebook.

"Where is the garden, Mr. Sykes?"

"It's on the other side of the hospital complex. Doctor Jefferson is in Umtali today picking up supplies but you could ask Sister Mukarakate to show you around. She has proven to be a fairly proficient gardener."

§

Samuel rode over to the hospital complex. This visit was not on his 'to do' list, but he knew it was necessary to follow where the investigation seemed to be leading.

The young nurse at the front desk asked him to sit down and wait a few moments while she went to call Sister Mukarakate. Five minutes later the nursing sister was proudly showing Samuel around the garden. The good lady knew most of the plants by name, and the garden had an excellent cross-section of both native and foreign plants, all neatly labelled with hand-written signs.

Thanks to Mrs. Pennefather, Samuel knew exactly what belladonna looked like. He could find none growing in the little garden, and when he questioned her, subtly, it was very obvious that Sister Mukarakate had absolutely no idea what he was talking about.

§

Charity was still living in the night-watchman's cottage behind the mission school, but it was clear that she was in the process of packing up her meagre possessions for the move back to her uncle's house in Umtali. Samuel could see cloth bundles tied up with hessian twine, and a dilapidated old cardboard suitcase, its latches no longer working, similarly secured with the same twine.

"*Mangwanani,* Charity. *Mararahere?*"

"I slept well if you slept well, uncle," the young girl responded politely, and walked over to where Samuel sat astride the Royal Enfield.

"Charity, I am very troubled by what has gone on here at the mission, and I think you know more about it than you are saying. Please, I am now very tired of going around in circles. I need answers today." And he slammed his right fist into the open palm of his left hand.

He hoped this much sterner attitude might push her into giving up that crucial piece of information that could possibly just crack this troubling case wide open.

The young girl looked up at him, her lips trembling. He sensed she was on the verge of saying something momentous, but then the moment passed, and she lowered her eyes again and said nothing.

"Charity! Look at me! Look into my eyes! We need to get to the bottom of this!"

The girl raised her head and looked at Samuel again, tears beginning to well in her limpid brown eyes. And then she began to talk.

"It was I, uncle, it was all my fault. Everything started with me and my stupid love for Gideon. He rejected me so many times. Please believe me, uncle, he was such a good, God-fearing man and a wonderful teacher. But I think I have already told you how an evil spirit, a *tokoloshe,* had got into me and I set my sights on him having me as a lover. The more he pushed me away, the more desperate I became. We were intimate only a few times at the kopje after I finished junior school and before I went off to live with my uncle in Umtali.

"The first time I had an opportunity to return was many months later and that is when I became pregnant. It happened late one evening. I went to his room in the staff quarters. I had seen another lady go to his room late at night and thought I could pass myself off as that same woman. His door was not locked and I entered very quietly and got into his bed. He was sleeping very deeply but I aroused him and we made love. After it was over he suddenly became wide awake and realised that I had tricked him; he was very, very angry.

"A few weeks later I realised I was pregnant. I told Gideon about it and although he was very angry at first, later he said that he would provide support for the baby and me, but I must tell no-one because he stood a great danger of being put in jail.

"Later, I told my other teacher, Isobel Takwanda, what had happened, asking her what could be done. She took me to see Doctor Jefferson at the hospital. He is too clever that man. Hau, after only one day I was no longer pregnant."

"But where did your grandfather come into it?"

"I can't be sure how he found out I was pregnant, perhaps he learnt it from Isobel, but he confronted me about it. It was a great shame to our family and he wanted the person responsible to pay compensation. I wouldn't tell him who the father was, only that he was a good man who would provide for the baby."

"So your grand-father went to the *ng'anga* for help with a divining tool?"

"Yes, my grandfather told me he had the means to find out who was the father of my unborn baby."

"And that divining tool was the warthog's tusk. Do you think your grandfather stabbed Gideon with the tusk?"

"No, it could not be him, uncle. His fingers could hardly hold a spoon to eat. His feet were also very painful so that he could only walk very slowly. And besides, the tusk was so curled that it would be impossible to stab anything with it. It could not have been my grandfather."

"No, you're probably right, but whoever did it must have known that your grandfather had the tusk and what he intended to use it for. Did you tell anyone else about the tusk and its purpose?"

Charity looked away, thinking.

"I think I told Isobel Takwanda. Yes, I am sure I did, for when I asked her for help I told her that my grandfather was very, very angry and had obtained some *mushonga* to find out who the father was."

"Thank you, Charity. When are you leaving here?"

"My uncle is coming to pick me up tomorrow. He has borrowed a motor-car from the post-master."

Samuel extended his hand. "Good luck, then, Charity, I wish you all the very best."

She shook his hand and curtsied, and Samuel wondered how things might have turned out if not for her unquenchable lust for an unavailable man. It seemed that her one final night of passion had unleashed a chain of events that had so far cost two lives.

§

Samuel left his motor-cycle on the roadway outside the school and walked up to the school administration block; Mr. Sykes called out from his office. "Mr. Kumalo, there is a telephone call for you. Umtali Hospital."

"Kumalo here, hello, can I help you." Samuel held the receiver to his ear.

"Yes, good morning, Samuel, Snelgar here. Sorry to phone you at the mission, but I thought it might be important. I phoned the mine and Eddie Evans told me where you had gone."

"It's fine, your timing was excellent, I have just arrived this minute at Mr. Sykes' office."

"Samuel, I received a cable back from my friend in Edinburgh. You know, the registrar of the medical school there?"

"Oh yes. The matter we spoke about yesterday?"

"Yes, exactly. Well he says that your medical friend left Edinburgh under a bit of a dark cloud."

"How so?"

"It seems he was suspected of performing illegal procedures in his digs, and it wasn't altruistic – he was doing it for money. My friend said he was very lucky not to have been charged by the police, but left for Rhodesia before they could get all the evidence together."

"These illegal procedures. Did he say what they were?"

"Abortions. It only came to light when one of his patients, if you could call her that, died. She was a fifteen-year-old prostitute. Oh, and there's something else you need to know about Lucas Hove's death."

§

Samuel found Isobel Takwanda in one of the class-rooms preparing for the new school year which was now only a few days away.

"Isobel. Good morning. Did you sleep well?"

"*Ndarara kana mararawo.*" They are *so* polite these Shona people, thought Samuel for what seemed the umpteenth time.

"Isobel, can you give me some time? I have a few questions."

Despite her polite answer to his greeting, she seemed petulant, and Samuel knew this was going to be a difficult interview.

"Isobel, please tell me what you know of Gideon's death. Were you present when he was murdered?"

"How can you ask me such a question? Why do you think I was there?"

"Well, I found a small white cotton handkerchief under the ironwood tree close to Gideon's body. Smaller than most normal handkerchiefs. It looks very, very similar to the handkerchiefs that you carry." And he pointed to a bulge under the hem of her dress sleeve.

"Show me that handkerchief, please."

Isobel reluctantly removed the small scrap of cotton from beneath her sleeve. He could see that she was rattled, her petulance beginning to dissolve.

The hankie she produced was identical to the one he had found under the ironwood tree. It was quite obviously home-made.

"This proves nothing. I could have been at the ironwood tree on another occasion."

"You are quite right, Isobel, you could have been, except for one thing. That hankie I found was lying on top of the dried leaves, and as we all know, the ironwood tree constantly sheds its leaves and its paper-like bark. So therefore, that hankie could only have been there for a few days before I found it."

Isobel was beginning to cry now and Samuel sensed they were now getting to the nub of the matter.

"So, Isobel, why were you there? And who was the murderer? Or was it you? The hankie evidence alone might be enough to convict you. This is a hanging matter, Isobel. Save yourself!"

"Me?" Her hands flew skywards, almost a supplication to the gods of sensibility. "I could not kill anybody, especially not Gideon; he was my friend, my fellow-teacher." She seemed frantic to convince Samuel of her innocence. He wondered if perhaps they were more than mere friends.

"Were the two of you lovers, Isobel?"

Now she really lost her composure, beginning to sob in huge gasps of air. Samuel didn't need her reply to know the answer.

"Yes," she finally answered, her eyes turned meekly to the grass beneath her feet, huge tears falling from her cheeks.

"So come on Isobel, you need to get this off your chest. You will feel so much better if you tell me the truth. Who killed Gideon?"

Isobel stood silently, her eyes not moving from the grass below her feet. She shuffled slightly then said, "It was Doctor Jefferson."

Samuel was astounded, not as to the how, for Jefferson certainly had the means and ability to kill both victims, but why? Why on earth would a man of healing resort to the murder of one man, possibly even two? Why?

"Doctor Jefferson? From the hospital? Why would he want to murder Gideon?"

"Because Gideon had found out about the abortions that the doctor was performing. Charity had told him. You see, Gideon was a very moral man, a true Christian. He believed that abortion is murder and went to confront Doctor Jefferson, threatened to expose him to the mission authorities. As you know, the mission is run by the American Methodists and they are very strict in their beliefs. Abortion is absolutely forbidden, and if they found out, Doctor Jefferson would be out of a job. Abortion is also against the civil law here in Rhodesia, so he would probably go to jail. Thus, Jefferson came to the conclusion that he had to kill Gideon to prevent him going to the authorities."

"But why over by the kopje under the ironwood tree? Why there particularly?" That damned kopje seems to have a great attraction as a lovers' meeting place, thought Samuel.

At this the young teacher's sobbing reached a higher level.

"That was our meeting place. Gideon was always afraid people would see me going to his room or vice versa, so we found this secluded place at the kopje. Doctor Jefferson told me to invite Gideon there on the night of his murder. He hid in the bushes and when Gideon came he hit him on the head with an iron bar. As he was lying on the ground he began to stab him with a curved, cream-coloured object."

"The warthog's tusk?"

"Exactly. First in the buttocks, and then he rolled him over and stabbed him in the groin. And then finally he took out a syringe and gave Gideon an injection into one of the wounds in his groin. He died very, very quickly."

"And what about Lucas, the old man, why kill him?"

"In a way that was my fault. I realised that I had mislaid my hankie and suspected that I may have left it at the kopje. I persuaded the doctor to accompany me to look for it early one morning before the sun came up. We couldn't find it, so I persuaded him to return again the following morning. Old Lucas must have seen our torch as we searched and he came up and challenged us. Doctor Jefferson already had a syringe ready and stabbed him in the stomach. Within five minutes the old man was dead."

"I think that syringe may have been intended for you, Isobel. Why else would he have been carrying it? He didn't know that Lucas would be coming near that place. I think you knew too much. You had better be careful from now on."

The truth of Samuel's statement suddenly dawned on her. Blood drained from her face and her fear became palpable. She looked over her shoulder more than once.

So there it was. Doctor Jefferson. The American dandy from Dallas, Texas, via Edinburgh, Scotland.

Evil personified. Two murders committed just to protect his reputation. And don't forget the fifteen year-old Princes Street prostitute. He could just imagine her bleeding to death in a squalid Leith bordello.

Just then Samuel heard a motor-cycle start up and roar away.

Chapter 20

Samuel sprinted back to Mr. Sykes' office to find the headmaster standing on the verandah looking bewildered.

"Where's my motor-cycle, Mr. Sykes? It was right here on the road outside your office. Did you see who took it?"

"Doctor Jefferson came to see me earlier on, said he'd heard you had been over at the hospital looking at the garden with Sister Mukarakate. He asked if I knew where you were now and I told him I thought you had walked over to see Charity, but then suddenly we heard you in the classroom talking to Isobel. It was then he jumped up and ran towards your motor-cycle and took off at high speed."

"Did he say where he was going?"

"No, he just said, 'I'll teach that interfering Matabele bastard' and then he was gone. It sounded as though he may have headed towards Penhalonga once he got to the mission gate."

"Do you have a car, Mr. Sykes? I need it very urgently. This is life or death." Samuel's thoughts were careening wildly through all the possibilities of what the crazed doctor might be thinking of doing in Penhalonga.

Sykes went to a board in the corner of his office and took down a small bunch of keys.

"There's a garage around the back of this building. Here are the keys. Do you know how to drive a Maxwell?"

"I can drive a Ford Model T, how different can it be?" and with that Samuel took the keys and ran.

§

The car was a four-door Maxwell Touring, a proud example of American industry, fairly new, and as Samuel was pleased to note, the petrol tank was almost full. It handled very well on the rutted road leading from the mission to Penhalonga. He had absolutely no idea where he would go once he reached Penhalonga, but thought that the words 'teach that Matabele bastard' sounded personal. He would go first to warn Agnes and send her and Hastings to her father's house. Farai should be fine where he was at Bella Evans' school. Once his family was safe then he would decide what to do next. He found it difficult to concentrate on more than one thought at a time.

Agnes was doing the family laundry in the big zinc tub, Hastings playing on the grass beside her. Samuel beckoned her to come over to the car, which she did only reluctantly, picking up Hastings and carrying the child on her hip, for her laundry was only half complete.

"What is it, my husband? Why do you bother me? You have your job and I have mine, and whewre did you get this car?"

215

"Get in the car woman, you are not safe here."

Something in his tone made Agnes realise that this was not a man in joking mode. She climbed awkwardly into the back of the four-seater vehicle hardly putting Hastings down before Samuel roared off to her father's house located a quarter mile away.

Screeching to a halt in a cloud of dust he shouted, *"Baba! Baba!"* loudly, not knowing whether the older man was there or not, but then out onto the verandah came Amos, his wife not far behind. "Go, Agnes," said Samuel. "Go to your father's house and do not let anyone in. No-one, you understand? Our family is in grave danger!"

Agnes could but nod her head in meek acknowledgement, for this was clearly not a time for lengthy explanations. She gathered Hastings in her arms and bolted out of the car and up the steps into the safety of her parents' house.

Samuel had no time to explain anything to his father-in-law, who stood there on the shady stoop, his mouth open in amazement as Samuel roared off in the big car. He probably thinks that I have kicked his daughter out of my house, thought Samuel, and smiled a little wryly. Nothing could be further from the truth. At this minute he had never loved his little family more.

And now to Bella's school, he thought. I'll just check on Farai and then start making other enquiries.

The children, all nine of them, were out in the schoolyard playing hop-scotch and tag when Samuel arrived. He ran up the school steps and through the open front door. Bella was seated at her desk and looked up in surprise.

"Samuel," she said, "what are you doing here? I was told that you were in Umtali and needed Farai for a witness statement."

"What! Who told you that?"

"That American doctor from the mission, er, Doctor Jefferson I think his name is."

"Did he take Farai?"

"Yes." And seeing the look of horror on Samuel's face said, "I thought it would be alright, I know you and Farai had been working together on the Revue case."

"Which way? Do you know which way they went?" He was struggling to keep his voice down and his emotions in check.

"No. But Elizabeth should know, she is outside supervising the children."

Samuel saw Elizabeth at the far end of the field, playing with a couple of the smaller children. He sprinted over to her. Four years earlier this same lady had been his and Hastings' cleaning lady when Hastings' ran the Penhalonga Police Station two doors down from the school. Now the station was closed temporarily, due to a shortage of man-power.

"Elizabeth, *masikati?* That man who took Farai. Did you see which way he went?"

"Is he a *tsotsi*, a bad man? I didn't like the look of him, but Bella said it was alright for Farai to go with him. He said you needed Farai in Umtali for a witness statement."

"Which way, Elizabeth?"

"Oh, sorry, he went that way," and she pointed north to where the main road disappeared in the direction of Inyanga and its high mountain ranges.

Samuel felt a sense of foreboding. How far could the doctor go without running out of fuel? He tried desperately to remember when last he had filled up the tank on the Royal Enfield. Yes. It had been the day before, and since then he had travelled about twenty miles on the machine. There should be sufficient fuel to get the motor-bike to Inyanga.

Samuel crashed the gear lever and sped off on the road to Inyanga. One consolation, he thought, is that people will definitely notice a speeding olive-green motor-cycle with an adult riding and a young lad behind on the pillion or, more probably, sitting in front on the fuel tank.

Samuel's first stop was at the general dealership owned by Mr. Dirubhai Patel, about twelve miles north of Penhalonga. Samuel knew that Patel stocked petrol, kept several forty-four gallon drums of the stuff, all marked 'Vacuum Oil' and with a red horse stencilled on the side.

Mr. Patel was standing on the store verandah when Samuel arrived. Above him was a vast array of brightly-coloured cotton dresses that hung on wire hangers from a steel rope that stretched from one side of the verandah to the other. At one end of the verandah sat Patel's tailor, his feet busy on the treadle of a Singer sewing machine.

"Constable Kumalo! What a surprise. We haven't seen you for so long. How are you? And how is your boss, Trooper Follett?"

"I am a civilian now, Mr. Patel. I was away at the war. I went with Mr. Follett, but unfortunately he was killed in action. He is buried in France."

"Oh, I am so sorry to hear that, he was such a nice young man.

"True, true," said Samuel, trying hard to hide his impatience with all this small talk. "Bur Mr. Patel I need to find someone, and I wonder if he stopped here or if you saw him pass by."

"Who?"

"It is a black man on an olive-green motor-cycle..."

"With a young black boy as a passenger?"

"Yes, the very one!"

"I saw them about a fifteen minutes ago heading north on the road towards Inyanga. They were travelling very fast – full speed!"

"Thanks Mr. Patel." And Samuel ran back to the Maxwell and roared off on the road north, wheels spinning in the loose gravel.

He had never been further north on this road than the turn-off to Frikkie Meyer's farm, and as he flashed by that turn-off he realized he was now in unfamiliar territory. All he knew was that this road led towards Inyanga and the Pungwe River. Why on earth Jefferson would want to head up into such remote country, Samuel had no idea, but he could think only of Farai and what danger he might be in.

§

And now Samuel could see the distinctive track of the Royal Enfield in the dirt road ahead of him. He was now in a deserted part of the world, hardly travelled at all by wheeled traffic. The Maxwell was a good car to drive, had lots of horsepower and handled well on these gravel roads. Occasionally Samuel passed a family on the road, perhaps leading a pack donkey, loaded down with sacks of maize or millet. But always his eye was on those Royal Enfield tracks as they bored inexorably onward.

Suddenly, at a road marked *Pungwe Gorge 12m*, the tracks veered off to the right but Samuel was going too fast to be able to turn in time. Cursing, he backed the car up, struggling at first to get it into reverse gear, the metal cogs in the gear-box grinding angrily. Then he was on his way again, but more carefully, for the road he was now on was narrow and the trees and bushes grew right into the track. Every now and again the sides of the car would resound with a thwack as a bush would hit one side of the car or the other.

Twelve miles can seem a hundred miles when you're anxious to reach your destination, but at the speed that

Samuel was going, they slipped away like telegraph posts alongside a railway track. The road ended abruptly in an open parking area, a large sign proclaiming *Pungwe Gorge Viewpoint*, and there beneath the sign was the Royal Enfield, its engine ticking as it cooled down after its frantic race from the mission.

"Mistuh Kumalo!" Samuel recognized Jefferson's voice calling from a distance. "Y'all are very persistent in yore pursuit. But you have come in vain, for I intend to head down this here river and straight over into Mozambique where y'all have no jurisdiction. And for insurance against any stupid action on your part, I have with me a young man to whom I believe you have taken quite a shine. Farai, the mission herd-boy."

Samuel couldn't make out where Jefferson was, but he could hear him clearly enough.

"Doctor Jefferson, why don't you just let Farai go free? I will do nothing to stop you leaving and heading down the Pungwe if you only send the boy back to me."

"Ha ha, you are a funny man, Kumalo. No sir, I rather like my insurance policy."

Now Samuel could hear a noise in the distance. It sounded like another motor vehicle coming at high speed towards him. And then there it was, a big black Dodge with a police sign on its roof, squealing to a halt in a cloud of dust. Barry Simcoe jumped out of the driver's side, while another three constables spilled from the other doors. Simcoe ran over to Samuel.

"Your cavalry's arrived," he said in a voice edged with high excitement.

"So glad to see you," said Samuel, "but how did you know?"

"Bella Evans phoned as soon as she realized that Farai had been kidnapped. So what's the story with the kidnapper? Who and why?"

"It's Doctor Jefferson from the Old Umtali mission hospital, and he's running because he's been exposed as the murderer of both Gideon and old Lucas."

"What! Are you serious? Doctor Jefferson? That smooth-looking American chap?"

"That's the very one, and right now he's over there." And Samuel pointed to a large, shady Flamboyant tree under which he had just seen some movement. "Now gather your men around, we're going to work out a plan."

§

The plan that Samuel devised was both simple and brilliant, incorporating the best of Sun Tzu's Art of War, a copy of which Samuel had been given to read by one of General Smuts' more enlightened, colour-blind, aide de camps in East Africa.

The momentum must be overwhelming, and the attack precisely regulated

He had the advantage of superior numbers, but he also had another advantage: a spy within the enemy camp. He could communicate with Farai in Chishona and he was pretty sure that Jefferson wouldn't understand a word.

"Farai!" he shouted in Shona, "we are going to be attacking from two sides, two men on your left and two on your right, while I will be attacking from the front. Do you understand, just say yes or no."

"*Hongu, baba.*" His high-pitched acknowledgement sounded confident, certainly not afraid, and Samuel took heart.

"As soon as we start attacking, when you hear the sound of us running, try to break free from that doctor and hide under a low bush or something. And try to act like a guinea-fowl hen on her eggs; do not move! Once we have dealt with him, we will come and look for you. We are starting now."

Samuel nodded at Barry and the other constables who were all well-versed in the plan of attack, to be centered on the large flamboyant tree. It was a classic rendition of the old Zulu 'bull's horns' tactic.

"Now!" whispered Samuel and everybody started sprinting towards their objective. Samuel moved rather more slowly than his support troops because he had less distance to cover and he wanted everybody to arrive at the same time.

A few seconds into the attack, Samuel heard a high-pitched yell from Farai and the sound of fast running through the low bushes. Now Jefferson was alone!

The five men converged on the Flamboyant tree almost simultaneously but Jefferson was gone, running along a path towards the Pungwe Gorge, a very deep ravine that starts almost at the source of the river on Inyangani Mountain. The Pungwe Falls, high above them, were a spectacular ribbon of white water tumbling down from the mountain and forming the river of the same name which then started to cut its way through the gorge on its way to the flatter land of Mozambique to the east. It was clear that Jefferson wanted to make it to the river and then follow the river eastwards into Mozambique, but he had misjudged the steepness of the gorge.

They could see him running along the lip of the gorge, looking back over his shoulder at his pursuers. One of the constables, a Manyika man who knew the area well, grabbed Samuel's arm.

"He will die if he continues running on that ridge," he said. "I know this area very well, and that ridge is always wet from the spray of the falls above and very muddy under the grass. It is treacherous. Many cattle and herd-boys have lost their lives here"

The men all came to a halt, breathing heavily as they watched Jefferson's progress.

Suddenly, almost without warning, the doctor uttered a cry and fell onto his backside. He clutched desperately at clumps of grass, and almost immediately began to slide over the edge of the gorge, disappearing from sight. The scream came to them on the wind, gradually diminishing in its intensity, until finally, inevitably, it abruptly ended.

"Come," said Samuel to the four policemen, "let's go and find Farai. I think I know where he is."

§

The Royal Enfield had but a small puddle of petrol remaining in its tank, and the Dodge was also close to empty. They had no means of siphoning fuel from the Maxwell, so, after hiding the bike under thatch in a copse of Msasa trees, and disabling the Dodge by removing the distributor cap, all six of them piled into the Maxwell, with Farai squished up between Samuel and Barry Simcoe, his legs separated by the long, floor-mounted gear stick.

"So come on, Samuel," said Barry, "tell us how you got to the bottom of the Gideon case? It must have happened all at once, because the last time I saw you, you had absolutely no idea."

"Well, I didn't know the *why* until I saw the teacher Isobel Takwanda one last time. But the *who*, well that I think I knew from the moment the *ng'anga* showed me the tusk, or at least the mate of the tusk, that he had given to Lucas to divine the man responsible for his grand-daughter's pregnancy.
"You see, the warthog has *two* sets of tusks, upper and lower. The upper ones are quite spectacular, almost circular, but also only intended for show, being otherwise fairly useless except to batter their male rivals in rutting season. It was this circular one, this symbol of virility, which the *ng'anga* had given to Lucas.

"Charity at some point must have told either Jefferson or Isobel, his lover, that her grand-father had obtained a warthog's tusk and was intent on using it to root out the father of Charity's unborn child. But since she had never seen it, she couldn't describe the tusk, only that it was from a warthog. When Jefferson wanted a tusk to use so as to deflect blame for Gideon's death on to Lucas, he sent Isobel to the Umtali Natural History Museum. She broke into their zoology exhibit, it wasn't locked, and she just took the first warthog's tusk she saw there. How could she have known that it was the wrong tusk?"

"And that was the lower tusk, the one that is always so sharp?"

"Exactly!"

"But why, Samuel? Why did Jefferson want to kill Gideon?"

"Not just Gideon. Lucas, too, remember."

"Yes, yes, but why?"

"It had to do with the abortions that Jefferson was doing at the hospital. His church is very much against the procedure from a religious point of view, and of course, you know that it is also against the civil law here in Rhodesia. Procuring an abortion can net you up to ten years in Salisbury Central Prison. Gideon had resigned himself to becoming a father, in fact was rather looking forward to it and had made arrangements to send a marriage-broker to talk to Charity's uncle to start *roora* proceedings. But Charity by then had had the abortion and informed Gideon of this fact. Apparently he hit the roof, was as mad as a jackal with rabies, and threatened to expose the good doctor.

"Isobel, whose name should really be Jezebel, lured Gideon to the ironwood *kopje* with promises of sex, and there waiting for him in the deep dark shadows of the ironwood tree was Doctor Jefferson. He laid Gideon down with a single blow from an iron bar, and then proceeded to stab him in backside and groin with the sharp tusk. He had brought along a hypodermic syringe and this he used to inject Gideon, within those same wounds, with a lethal dose of potassium cyanide."

"Alright, that I understand, but why kill the old man Lucas?"

"I regret to say that I am, in a way, partially responsible for his demise. You see, I had found a small white hankie at the scene of Gideon's murder. It had been misplaced by Isobel. She knew she had mislaid it and was desperate to find it, but of course, you had it, Barry, logged in as evidence. But she didn't know that.

"The two of them, she and the doctor, returned to the *kopje* with flashlights to try and find the missing hankie and Lucas must have seen the lights. In fact, his observations are in his report for that night. I have a copy of that page for your evidence file, Barry, although it now seems fairly redundant.

"Of course, no hankie could be found, so they went back again early the next morning for another look, and this time

Lucas came right up to them, wanting to know what they were doing. Jefferson stabbed him with a hypodermic syringe in the lower abdomen, within the pubic hairline, almost impossible to see in an autopsy. The syringe this time contained Belladonna which, in excess, can cause the heart to race uncontrollably. In an old person it would be fatal, an unexpected bonus for the doctor. You see, I believe he had taken the syringe along with him to do away with Isobel, for, like Gideon, she knew too much. But that is something we will never know. Jefferson had obtained the Belladonna from Mrs. Pennefather's garden through Mr. Sykes, the mission school headmaster, who was totally oblivious to Jefferson's motives.

"And there you have it, Barry, what I like to refer to as the case of the Warthog's Tusk. Two promising young men, one good, one evil, cut down before their prime. And I still have to tell Gideon's mother exactly what happened to her son." Samuel paused, a wry smile on his lips.

"There is one last thing for you to do, Barry. Send a letter to the Edinburgh City Police in Scotland. They have an open file on a deceased 15-year-old prostitute, an abortion that went wrong. Tell them that they can close their file, their prime suspect is dead."

The End